AGENT PROVOCATEUR

CHARLES BISHOP #2

DAVE SINCLAIR

AGENT PROVOCATEUR

Bishop returns, and this time it's personal.

When Bishop's former mentor threatens to instigate a nuclear war, the MI6 agent dives headlong into a deeply personal mission where nothing is quite what it seems.

Racing across China with enemy hounds snapping at his heels, Bishop is forced to confront not only a relentless adversary, but also demons from his own past.

Full-throttle action, snappy dialogue and twists at every turn, *Agent Provocateur* will have you turning pages late into the night.

NOTE TO THE READER

Note to the reader: Although the Bishop novels can be read in any order, the events described in this book take place after those in *Kiss My Assassin.*

Dedicated to my sister, Alli.

Who I felt in no way obligated to dedicate this book to after she dedicated her last book to me. Especially since I dedicated my last book to the cat.
Anyway, I'm still not apologising for when I was fourteen and turned the power off to the house when you were listening to The Cure. Fight me.

PROLOGUE

The gun appeared real enough.

Chaun grasped his stick. It was his favourite—just the right length, with a good handle to grip. It took an effort to push the pistol across the dirt with his trusty stick. The weapon was heavy, not plastic. That meant it was real. Chaun had never seen a real gun before. In movies, sure, but never in real life.

He glanced about the village. No one else was around. Chaun's father and uncle had left at first light to tend to the rice fields, like they did every day. His mother and her sisters were washing and exchanging gossip about village life, most of which Chaun didn't understand. Through the reeds, he could hear his mother saying that her youngest sister, Mei Lien, was sleeping around. The other women seemed to find this most distressing. Chaun didn't see the problem. He often felt tired, and wouldn't mind sleeping around all the time. Adults were weird.

He knew he should call his mother and show her the gun. But as he opened his mouth, Chaun stopped. He would probably get into trouble again. Somehow it would be his fault a pistol had appeared in the middle of the village road. He'd be sent to bed without supper, just like he had been the day before, all because he'd brought a dead bird into the house. His mother brought dead things into the house all the time, but apparently a raven was different to a chicken.

Staring longingly at the weapon, Chaun decided to leave it where it lay. Someone else would find it, and they could get into trouble. Yes, that was exactly what he needed to do. It was too early in the day for him to be told off. He had exploring to do.

He wandered down to the stream, whacking his stick on trees as he went. Once he reached the water he considered skipping stones again, but dismissed the idea. He'd done it a thousand times. He was the best stone skipper in the village. He wished he had a sibling to compete against, but Chaun had to entertain himself. As the other kids in the village thought he was weird. It wasn't his fault. They were amused by rolling a metal hoop up and down the hill. Chaun wanted more.

He couldn't stop thinking about the gun. He imagined himself shooting trees and birds. Chaun had seen more films than anyone else, so he would obviously be the best marksman in the village. Last year his cousin had introduced him to movies, and the seven-year-old was immediately smitten. The other worlds, the feverish pace, the excitement was nothing like his life. His cousin, Jie, was away at boarding school in Wuwei and wouldn't be back for weeks. Chaun hoped he'd bring new movies with him. His favourite movie star was Tom Cruise. Chaun had seen all the *Mission Impossible* films. There was always a lot of running. So much running.

Hefting a big rock into the stream, he watched the spurt of water as it landed, and counted the ripples. Chaun was certain of one thing. He was bored. He was probably the most bored kid in all of China. Possibly the world.

Across the stream, Chaun heard popping noise. No, not popping, more of a metallic *clack clack* sound. Nothing in the village made a *clack clack* sound. Chaun lifted his head, trying to see what was making the strange noise.

Hearing a rustle, he turned to see a dark figure flit through the reeds. Face obscured, the figure moved fast, frequently turning his head as if being chased. The parting reeds moved towards where Chaun stood. Unable to move, the boy watched the figure with a mixture of fear and excitement. He was no longer the most bored kid in China.

The figure sprinted out of the reeds and staggered when he hit the thick mud on the other side of the stream. Chaun gasped.

It was the first Western man he'd ever seen in person. The man had a serious face, and the grey of his beard made him appear distinguished, unlike his grandfather, who looked like an old mop left outside in the rain. He wore a white shirt and a black jacket. There were red blotches on his shirt. Was it blood?

Chaun's eyes focused on the item in the man's hands. It was a gun, just like the one he'd seen on the road. The man didn't seem to not have noticed Chaun.

He turned and fired. The sound wasn't like in the movies. In the movies, guns make *loud* sounds, big booming heroic noises. This was more of a pop. Chaun was a little disappointed.

There was someone else coming through the reeds. Suddenly a man in a Chinese army uniform appeared, staggering. He lurched, clutching his chest, and fell forward into the stream. He didn't move. *Why isn't he moving?* Rivulets of dark red liquid leaked into the clear water of the stream.

Chaun didn't think it was heroic like in the movies. The soldier just fell. No big cry, no flailing arms. He just flopped on the ground and stayed there. Unsure what to think, Chaun frowned and stared, waiting for him to get up.

The Western man glanced about and his eyes fell on Chaun. Angry shouts came from the direction the man had run from. More soldiers. The Westerner grinned and gave Chaun a nod. He placed his index finger to his lips. *Shhhh.*

That was when Chaun noticed the case in the man's hand. It was yellow plastic, with a handle, like the brief-cases he'd seen in the movies. Something else he'd seen in movies was the symbol on the side: a triangle, with a yellow and black circle design. That meant hazard. Maybe nuclear danger? Did the man have a nuclear bomb in his case? Chaun decided it was the coolest thing he'd ever seen.

The man leapt across the stream towards him. He was shorter than Chaun had expected. Not like Tom Cruise. Tom must be a mountain, he looked so tall on the big screen. The Westerner walked straight-backed and proud, like Chaun's grandfather had tried to make him do. He'd never quite succeeded.

The man crouched next to Chaun and gave him a wink. He had a friendly face, like someone you could play checkers with and they wouldn't cheat. Up close, Chaun could see that he had wrinkles, and his beard had more grey hairs than black. If Chaun was to guess, the man was old. Really old. Like, over thirty or something.

Now that he was standing in front of him, Chaun noticed more red on the man's shirt. If this was a movie, it would definitely be blood. It really seemed like a movie.

More shouting, louder this time. The soldiers were close. There seemed to be a lot of them. The man stood, as if ready to leave. His gaze focused on the mill. With a nod, he took a step in that direction. Before Chaun realised what he was doing, his hand darted out and grasped the Westerner's forearm. He shook his head.

Slowly, he pointed to the right, through the barn leading to the railyard. That's where Chaun would go. The man smiled and nodded. He patted him on the head gratefully. He gripped the gun in one hand and the case in the other. Then the odd Westerner crouched, and broke into a run.

Just like Tom Cruise.

CHAPTER ONE

There are different types of hangovers. There's the slightly dehydrated but functional kind. There's the death warmed up, feel marginally better after an industrial-sized coffee and a greasy toasted sandwich kind. Then there was Bishop's current state, which could be succinctly classified as the DEFCON 1 of hangovers. The kind where one vows never to drink again, and actually believes that they won't.

Lying on his kitchen floor, the cool tiles momentarily soothed the vice-like pressure on the sides of Bishop's aching skull. He couldn't even remember how he'd managed to crawl there. It must have been a wild night. The only details he remembered were wearing a sombrero and a vague recollection of jumping into a fountain for reasons that presently eluded him. There was definitely a mariachi band in there somewhere. Everything else was fuzzy.

Bishop had made the most of his extended leave of absence after his last mission. He'd needed the recovery time. Unfortunately, after the first half hour he'd become deathly bored. Four weeks in, he was close to madness.

Being a civilian wasn't for him—he wasn't built for a sedentary life. Patiently waiting in line at the Tesco deli lacked the thrill of someone shooting at him. He was an MI6 field agent through and through. Bishop craved action.

Just not at this precise moment in time.

Right now, he desired stillness and silence. In his sensitive state, the low hum of the fridge sounded like a jet engine. Even the paint was painfully loud.

As if reading his thoughts, the silence was shattered by the doorbell. Fighting nausea, Bishop lifted his head and tried to focus on the clock on his Miele oven. 9:01 am. Admittedly, it was a respectable time for someone to be calling on him. He just wished it was on a different day. Ignoring it didn't seem to make much of a difference; the third set of ringing clinched it. The only way to stop the incessant noise was to answer the damn door.

Peeling himself off the floor, Bishop groaned to his feet and clutched the fridge for stability. Fighting the nausea that enveloped him, he dragged his feet across to the rich red carpet of his lounge. Normally he took great pride in his collection of vintage travel posters, antiques and leather-bound books. Not today. Today he was focused on not throwing up.

After flicking the various locks, Bishop gripped the handle and inhaled deeply to steady himself. The moment was shattered by another buzz of the doorbell. Frustrated, he wrenched the door open, ready to give the harbinger of his irritation a spray.

But he didn't.

The words fell from his lips and shattered, unuttered, on the floor. He stared, aware he should be blinking but unable to summon the requisite energy. Gobsmacked was a good word for it. Flabbergasted was another. Knowing he should say something, Bishop searched his slugging brain for an appropriate greeting. Something erudite and adroit.

"Sweet son of a fuck."

Raising an eyebrow, the party on the other side of the door tilted her head. "I don't know how to respond to that." Beneath her shaggy short brown hair, Tessa shrugged. "That's not me being nice, I actually don't know how to respond."

Although aware that his mouth was hanging open, Bishop didn't care. *She* was standing in his doorway. Capital S She. If he were given to clichés—he wasn't—he would call her the love of his life. The one he had thrown his entire soul into. The one who had crushed his heart like the centre of a collapsing supernova.

He wasn't in the mental space for this. He didn't believe he'd ever be in the mental space for this. Bishop stared.

With a tilt of her head, Tessa said, "Aren't you going to invite me in?"

"I've seen way too many vampire movies to think that's a good idea."

"You're being preposterous, Charles." Tessa moved to walk inside and regarded him inquisitively.

Bishop stepped aside. "Fine, but I warn you, I have a stake."

"I thought you were a vegetarian."

Tessa walked in, shrugging off her coat, and tossed it onto the Eames lounge chair by the door, just as she'd done a million times before. Although not for two years, since she'd walked out for the last time. Or at least, what he'd thought was the last time.

"Oh marvellous," Bishop rubbed his temple as he shut the door, "we're doing banter."

Strolling into the centre of the lounge, Tessa did a 360

to take in the room. "Still embracing the gentlemanly bordello aesthetic, I see."

Over their five-year relationship she'd tried several times to get him to change the classic blood red wallpaper and decor, but he'd held strong. At the time, he'd thought he was clinging to what he saw as the last bastion of his individuality, his apartment. Unbeknown to him, that wasn't where the problem lay.

In an effort to end the waking nightmare as fast as possible, Bishop asked, "Why are you here, Tessa? Did Satan buy a snowplough?"

Not answering him directly, she extended her neck and examined the various doors leading off the lounge.

With a crinkled forehead, Bishop asked, "Looking for ninjas?"

Continuing her stationary exploration, Tessa didn't look at him. "No, just harlots."

Bishop rolled his eyes. "I assure you, your estimation of my current lifestyle is not only erroneous, it is, quite frankly, offensive."

From behind the closed door of the bathroom, a toilet flushed. There was the sound of a running tap, then a short buxom woman emerged in skimpy underwear and shrieked. Attempting to cover herself—and failing comprehensively—she crab-walked to the bedroom and slammed the door behind her.

Tessa turned to Bishop and raised an eyebrow.

He shrugged and issued a roguish grin. "If nothing else, you have to admit it was awesome timing."

Leaving his ex standing in the centre of the lounge, Bishop followed the young lady into the bedroom. In quick order, he apologised for the surprise, helped her find her dress, sent her on her way with a taxi fare and promised to call her later.

After closing the front door, Bishop realised he didn't

know her name. Feeling a chill, he slipped on his brown dressing gown. The sound of clanging cutlery pulled him towards the kitchen. Tessa leaned against the bench, two cups of coffee in hand. She handed one to Bishop without comment.

The odd thing was the guilt he felt about Tessa seeing the woman. Was her name Grace? Maggie? Something like that. It had been two years; Tessa had no right to expect him to have remained celibate. Yet he had no wish to see her upset. If he were honest, he still cared.

He took a sip of the coffee and felt marginally revived. He thought it telling that she still remembered he had his coffee black. The woman before him was at once so familiar and so foreign. He recalled every curve of her beautiful face, but it seemed like it was from another time, another life.

Tessa nodded towards the front door. "She seemed nice." The smirk on her soft lips and the upward inflection of her tone might as well have been an extremely large arrow pointing to her head saying "liar!"

Bishop chuckled. He wasn't going to engage in that particular discussion. He nodded in her direction. "Your hair's nice short. Suits you."

"Thanks." A genuine smile crossed her lips. She assessed him, from his bare feet to his unkempt hair. "You look… actually, you look like crap, Charles." As if surprised by what she'd said, she quickly added, "Uh, no offence."

Bishop's face creased into an amused smirk. "How could I possibly be offended by that?"

For the first time in years, they shared a laugh. She'd always had a killer laugh. If you heard it from across the room, you couldn't help smiling. She had a unique ability to light up a room with her mere presence. Memories came flooding back, but Bishop stamped them down. He needed all his brain power to stand and breathe at the same time.

Bishop motioned that they should move back to the lounge and sit on the couch. Sitting was easier. Before they sat, he moved aside a sombrero.

"I assume you weren't just passing. What's this about, Tessa?"

"Dad."

The word almost made Bishop spit out his coffee. Out of all the reasons Tessa could possibly have for turning up on his doorstep unannounced, Tessa's father would have to be the most unlikely.

"What about Kevin?"

"Have you heard from him?"

"Tessa," Bishop placed his coffee on the table to show she had his full attention. "I haven't heard from your father in years, you know that. Kevin hasn't spoken to me since..."

Bishop let the words trail off. They both knew how the sentence ended. Tessa's father hadn't spoken to his former apprentice since he'd run off with his daughter. Kevin Argento had been Bishop's mentor for years. He'd guided him from the SAS into MI6. But their supposedly unbreakable bond had shattered the day Bishop fell in love with his daughter.

"He's missing?"

Tessa nodded, her eyes moist. Her bottom lip quivered. It was one of the few times he'd seen her so vulnerable. "Six weeks he's been gone. Took a trip and just vanished. Nobody has heard from him. No notes. Hasn't touched his bank accounts. Nothing."

Shifting in his seat, trying to process the information with a less than fully functional brain, Bishop attempted to come up to speed. It wasn't easy.

"Where was the trip?"

"Sorry?"

"You said he took a trip and disappeared."

Tessa glanced at her hands and avoided his eyes. "China."

Bishop baulked. "China? That's the last place I'd ever expect him to be, not after—"

Tessa's head snapped around and Bishop caught himself before he said the name. She obviously felt pain at her father's disappearance, she didn't need to be reminded of more hurt.

Bishop hastily changed tack. "Why would he contact me?"

"To be honest, I don't think he would." She ran her fingers through her hair. "But I've tried everyone else. You think I'd be here if I wasn't absolutely desperate?"

The words shouldn't have stung, but they did. He chose to focus on the subject at hand.

"If there's anyone on this planet more able to look after themselves, I'd like to meet them. Your father is the single most capable man I've ever known."

Her hands flew into the air. "Then why has he disappeared?"

"Tessa, I don't know."

She nodded, as if accepting his answer. Half raising her head, she gazed in his direction but failed to meet his eyes. "Would you… would you be able to help me? To find him?"

There it was. It had been two years, but Bishop could still read his former lover. She could have texted him to ask if he'd heard from her father. There was more to it. That she couldn't meet his eye told him she was embarrassed to ask. She was a proud woman.

"Tessa, I don't know if that's such a good idea."

"You have the resources, surely. Call in a few favours,

that kind of thing. If what we once had means anything to you…"

"Woah, that escalated quickly."

"He's missing, Charles! What else can I do?" Her voice reached a pitch he'd rarely heard. She calmed herself and continued. "You know him better than anyone. You could check records, see if he's left China, checked into a hotel… something. Anything."

The desperation in her tone was obvious. The woman who sat before him cradling her coffee was at her wits' end.

"Tessa, utilising MI6 resources to find a man who as far as I know isn't in danger would not only get me fired, it would likely have me hauled in front of the Intelligence and Security Committee, too." He lowered his tone when Tessa's face fell, but continued. "That's a huge ask. Maybe if I knew more about why he went to—"

"So you're refusing to help." Her words were hard. Her expression matched them.

"Tessa, I didn't say that. I said I need some context. Like, what—"

"I knew this was a waste of time." She slammed the coffee cup down and threw her hands in the air. "I'm sorry to have intruded."

She moved to stand, but before she did Bishop placed his hand on her arm. Instead of aggravating her, the gesture calmed her. Composing herself, she nodded.

In a far gentler voice, she said, "This was wrong. I shouldn't have come. I'll go. Sorry to have disturbed your… whatever."

They stood, and Bishop fought the nausea that came with the motion.

As she approached the door, he saw the pain in her eyes. That was unlike her. Tessa wasn't one to give in to her emotions. Bishop had once joked that he thought she was half Vulcan. She truly was rattled, desperate.

She paused at the threshold and turned, her face softer, more like he remembered. "I'm sorry for barging in like this, it's just that Dad…"

"It's okay, Tessa." He placed a hand on her shoulder; she didn't flinch. "If I hear anything, I'll call you straight away, okay?"

She nodded, pursing her lips in a feeble attempt at a smile. "Thanks."

"Actually, Tessa, one last thing."

She glanced up, eyes curious.

"Do you want a sombrero?" He lifted the hat. "I don't really need another one."

She shook her head and the faintest trace of a grin broke through. "You're an idiot."

"Well, at least you know some things haven't changed."

She rolled her eyes and touched his cheek. As if only just realising what she was doing, she retracted it quickly, shoving her hand in her pocket.

"If you hear anything at all…"

"I still have your number."

She nodded. Tessa stepped into the hallway and walked away, not looking back. Bishop closed the door and leaned against it for support. He noted that his hands were shaking. It wasn't the drink.

A million times he'd dreamt of seeing her again. He'd spent months imagining going back in time, changing events, somehow stopping their downward spiral. It took a long time, but Bishop had eventually realised that wallowing in self-pity and what-ifs wasn't going to change a damn thing. Nothing would. She wasn't coming back.

Then suddenly, she did.

It was going to take some time for him to process what had just happened. Seeing her again was both painful and joyous, and her distress over her father made it hard to differentiate one churning emotion from another.

He'd spend time sifting through it all, but later. Right now Bishop needed to chug a few litres of water and lie down for a decade or two. He glanced outside. It was a beautiful autumn day. London in autumn was his favourite place to be, though he suspected the remainder of his day would be spent inside nursing the mother of all hangovers.

Before swallowing all the recovery vitamins and water he could lay his hands on, Bishop ran a bath. He'd likely spend the rest of the day in there, perhaps the week. Glancing through the bathroom window, he saw Tessa step onto the footpath and wrap a figure-hugging coat around her. It was the first chilly day of the year. She headed south towards Oxford Circus station. He'd always loved watching her walk away. She had a way of swinging her hips that he found utterly captivating. Good to see there were other things that hadn't changed.

Turning to head to the kitchen for water, Bishop noticed two men walking in the same direction as Tessa. They were on opposite sides of the street, but both kept the same pace. What drew his attention was the laser focus each of the black-coated men had on Tessa. She was an attractive woman, stares were common, but these two weren't admiring her walk.

Both men were Asian in appearance. Not one for racial profiling, Bishop was close to dismissing the men's presence as a mere coincidence. But then one spoke into his sleeve and the other nodded. That clinched it. Tessa was being followed.

Bishop flung open the door and raced down the stairs,

gown fluttering behind him. His aching head screamed in protest. Bounding onto the street, he took after Tessa and her pursuers. *Supposed pursuers*, he reminded himself. He recalled a phrase he'd heard long ago: "circumstantial evidence is still evidence". Like a slap in the face, he realised it was one of Tessa's father's sayings.

With great strides, Bishop caught up with the two men, now on the same side of the street as Tessa. He passed them, not giving them a sideways glance. In no time he was stride for stride beside Tessa. Mouth agape, her eyes went wide at his sudden appearance.

Before she spoke, Bishop cut her off. In a low voice he said, "You've got a tail."

"You've got a nice one too, but that doesn't mean you get to accost me in the street, Charles."

Bishop stared at her blankly as they walked. "I don't know if you're being cute or clever."

"Can't I be both?" Her grin was wide. Tessa's features turned serious. "I noticed them half a block back. Been watching them in shop windows ever since. You have a play?"

Bishop could have been shocked at her sudden change in demeanour, but wasn't. It was one of the reasons he'd fallen in love with her. She could be vulnerable, cute and commanding all at the same time. She'd morphed from sombre dejection to playful readiness in mere seconds. He almost pitied her pursuers.

When Bishop turned, he noticed that one had split off, leaving the other close behind. It was too early to tell if that was a good thing or not.

Tessa assessed him. "I'm going to be honest, I've seen you better prepared."

Bishop realised he was barefoot, unarmed and dressed for bed. "Are you saying my tactical dressing gown is inappropriate attire?"

"I'm saying there's no such thing as a tactical dressing gown."

Passing a toy shop window, Bishop saw the reflection of the remaining pursuer speaking intensely into the mic in his wrist. He quickened his pace. Bishop's sudden appearance had modified their plans, but he hadn't broken off. That meant they required something urgently from Tessa. All the more reason for Bishop to be concerned.

Bishop was about to suggest they duck into a local pub where he knew the owner when the other pursuer stepped onto the street 20 metres ahead. He was short of breath, having run around the block to cut them off. The one behind slowed his pace, openly smiling.

The gent in front—heavy set, probably in his early forties—tilted his head. With a nod in Tessa's direction, in perfect English he said, "Ms Argento, I was wondering if we could have a word." He paused to evaluate Bishop. "Alone." As if to emphasise his position on the matter, he opened his jacket to reveal a holstered gun.

If the man had expected Tessa to be intimidated by the sight, he was sorely mistaken. The daughter of a Brigadier of the 21st Special Air Service Regiment had seen a gun before. Many, in fact. Confusion creased the man's face, as if perplexed by the lack of reaction. He eyed the gun tucked under his jacket, as if to confirm it was still there.

As cool as a frozen cucumber, Tessa replied, "Terribly sorry, old chap, I'm afraid I have a train to catch."

She went to move around him, but the man stepped sideways to block her. "I really must insist."

The man was now standing centimetres from Tessa. The one behind focused exclusively on Bishop. Everyone tensed. They all knew where this was headed. Bishop untied the cord from around his dressing gown and without looking down, fashioned it into an impromptu noose.

Tessa sighed. "Insist all you want," she glanced back at Bishop, fire in her eyes, "but unless you intend on using that thing, we're done here."

The man stared blankly. It wasn't the reaction he'd expected. Bishop smirked. If the guy had wanted a typical reaction, he'd chosen the wrong woman. He forced his hazy mind to focus. The hangover was doubling down but he did his best to keep his head in the game. Last night's heavy drinking was unlikely to help him, unless he could breathe on his opponents. Their comms equipment and strategic positioning told him that these guys were trained. They couldn't be underestimated.

Extracting the pistol, the man aimed it at Tessa's chest. The QSW-06 suppressed pistol was standard issue for the People's Liberation Army. If these guys were indeed Chinese, Bishop thought it the epitome of arrogance to assume they could brandish their own weapon unchallenged. Or perhaps it was necessity that drove them to make such a mistake. Possibly both.

Bishop crouched, readying himself like a spring. His head pounded but he shut it out. As quietly as he could, he said, "Ready."

Almost imperceptibly, Tessa nodded. Addressing the man before her, she said, "Mighty brave of you to whip that out on the street. Anyone can see you."

As the lead man turned his head to check the street, Tessa struck. Her left hand darted out and drove the gun upward instantaneously. She twisted the weapon as she propelled her right fist forward and punched his left hand away.

Bishop swivelled and attacked the man at his rear. He grasped the man's jacket and yanked either side down, pulling him close. The net effect was that the man was unable to move his arms. Bishop headbutted him and regretted it instantly. His brain screamed, *this is not helping your hangover, mate!*

Ignoring his surging nausea, Bishop looped the cord of his dressing gown over the man's head and pulled down hard. His head careened forward, meeting the blunt force of Bishop's fist. As he drew back, Bishop yanked again, so head and fist crunched together once more. He heard a satisfying snap, likely the man's nose cartilage.

Bishop turned to Tessa, who was wrestling with her attacker. She continued to twist the gun away, jabbing her fingers into the joints of his hand. With a shriek, the man relinquished the weapon. It wasn't a clean move, but it worked.

Aiming the weapon at the man's head, Tessa panted heavily. "You alright?" she asked Bishop.

Bishop rubbed his forehead. "Yeah, fine. Remind me next time not to headbutt anyone when I have a hangover."

Bishop still had the man on the end of the cord, like a dog on a leash, his arms still pinned by the jacket. Every time he struggled, Bishop yanked the cord and delivered a blow. The man's partner was similarly stymied. Any chance of a counterattack was dashed now that Tessa held the gun. There was surprise in the man's expression. He should have known better. Of course the daughter of an SAS soldier would know how to defend herself.

"Bloody hell, my karate is a bit rusty." She gave Bishop a half smile. "Think I pulled… everything."

"I think you did exceptionally—"

"Hold it right there!"

They turned to see a constable with terror stretched across her young face. In one hand she held an extended

ASP baton, in the other, a can of CS spray, aimed in their direction.

"Metro Police. Put the gun down, now!"

Tessa threw the gun to the ground as if it were electrified.

Frowning, Bishop said, "Please stop shouting. You're very loud and I've had a rough morning."

"Let him go, sir. I'm warning you."

Bishop nodded towards the officer, smiling. He jerked the man at the end of his impromptu leash and punched him in the face.

"Oi, stop that!" The officer aimed the CS spray at Bishop.

He nodded. "Right you are, Officer." He proceeded to punch the man again.

"Oi!" The officer took a step forward, pushing the spray closer to Bishop's face.

Relinquishing his grip with a face as innocent as three-day-old puppy, Bishop stepped back. The man he'd been punching staggered, shaking his head, punch drunk. The two assailants gawped at one another in silence. And then, as if on cue, they sprinted in different directions, Bishop's foil comically running away with his jacket around his arms and a dressing gown cord around his neck.

The lone constable yelled after them to stop, but Bishop understood why she didn't chase them down. She was obliged to focus on the main threat, and right then and there, that was the person who had been holding the gun. There was no time to explain, and the men were soon out of sight.

"Stay where you are!" The young constable's voice trembled, but the spray in her hand didn't waver. She was tough. Bishop liked her.

Raising his hands, he nodded down the street. "Look, I understand what this appears like, but if I could just—"

Bishop made to walk away, but the officer shook her head. "No you bloody don't, mate."

"But I left the bath running."

The constable remained stony-faced.

Bishop squinted. "Fine. But just so you know, the people in the apartment downstairs are going to be really pissed in about five minutes."

As the constable cautiously approached, mumbling into her lapel mic about backup, Bishop turned to Tessa.

"Who were those guys?"

Wringing her hands and trying to calm her breaths, Tessa shook her head. "I... I don't know."

"You think it's related to your father?"

"I bloody well hope not." She regarded him carefully. The softness of her gaze reminded him of the Tessa he remembered. "Otherwise he's in a hell of a lot more danger than I thought."

CHAPTER TWO

"Welcome back."

Bishop's boss, Paul, extended a hand over his large mahogany desk. He greeted his subordinate and friend with a wide grin, and motioned for Bishop to sit.

Although keen to discuss the events of the previous day, Bishop held back. His boss always had an agenda. He'd learned long ago to let Paul steer the conversation.

"You're looking well rested."

You should have seen me yesterday, Bishop thought with a smirk. Running around the streets of London fighting off attackers with the mother of all hangovers was not conducive to appearing one's best.

Bishop said, "Thanks boss, eager to get back to it." He wasn't lying.

Paul steepled his fingers and nodded. "I know we wanted to ease you in slowly after Haiti, but things have taken a rather urgent turn. We need to send you back into the field sooner than we thought."

"Fine by me." Bishop sat up. "My bathroom needs a whole mess of repairs, so that should work out nicely."

Paul's posture was unnatural for the big, lumbering

man. He shifted uneasily. Whatever he was about to say clearly made him uncomfortable.

"This one's a bit, ah, personal I'm afraid."

Something was off. Bishop didn't know what yet, but Paul's hesitancy put him on edge. "Personal how?"

"We have a rogue ex-MI6 agent going around killing foreign agents in their homes. We've just received word that he's upgraded to trying to kill politicians."

Ex-MI6? Bishop's stomach turned to ice. "These foreign agents... they wouldn't happen to be Chinese, would they?"

For an uncomfortably long time, Paul stared at Bishop. He made no noise, but blinked incessantly. Finally, his lips parted. "How in the ruddy hell did you know that?"

"Given what occurred yesterday and the fact that you're sending me on an urgent personal mission, I just assumed..."

"Wait, wait," Paul rubbed his temples, "yesterday?"

It was Bishop's turn to stare. "The JIC didn't contact you, did they?"

Slowly, Paul shook his head. "Perhaps you should start at the beginning."

Bishop gave Paul a rundown of the last twenty-four hours: Tessa, the men who had followed her and the hours spent convincing the police that they were the victims, not the aggressors.

He was careful to omit how spending time with Tessa had made him feel. The woman had been his everything once. Since she'd walked out of his life for what he'd thought was the last time, he'd built a wall of ice around his heart. No woman came close to penetrating the shield he'd built to protect himself. And then suddenly, *she* was there. The day before he'd fought a constant battle between nostalgia, resentment, the immediate danger and the need to protect the woman who had shattered him so. She could still confound him, even after all this time.

There was no need to mention any of this to his boss. For one thing, it was personal and irrelevant to the mission. Second, as his friend, Paul would know exactly what he was going through. He'd helped Bishop pick up the pieces after Tessa left.

When he'd finished bringing his boss up to speed, Bishop leaned forward. "Am I to assume this rogue ex-agent is Kevin Argento?"

"I'm afraid so, yes."

Bishop inhaled deeply, then exhaled. "I'm going to need a moment."

Mind racing, he tried to process this information. Tessa's father, his former mentor, the man who had plucked Bishop from the SAS and recruited him into MI6 was, what, a killer? An assassin? It didn't make sense. None of it made sense.

"I can't see it. Kevin retired to the country. He breeds ducks and watches Miss Marple. There's obviously been some kind of—"

"There's footage of him fleeing an assassination." Paul cut him off. He sat upright and tugged at his vest. "I'm sorry Bishop. It's clear cut. The Chinese are threatening all-out war on this. They're mobilising. Their alert status is the highest it's been since Tiananmen Square. Three hundred nukes have been loaded into launchers. The Royal Navy have tracked their aircraft carrier leaving Jianggezhuang Naval Base on the Yellow Sea. This is turning very bad, very quickly. Kevin Argento has declared a one-man war against China."

"I think he's outnumbered."

Paul didn't seem to find the quip amusing. "The fact

that he's taken out as many targets as he has without being caught shows how dangerous the old bastard is."

Still processing, Bishop tried to make light of it. "That can't be right. You can't have a supervillain called Kevin. Scaramanga, sure. Deatheater 2000, absolutely. But not Kevin. Kevin's someone who does your taxes, not someone who starts a war."

His superior did not seem to appreciate the humour. In fact, his face grew graver still. "No one in the Service knows him better than you, Bishop. You know how he thinks, how he reacts, his tactics. I'm sorry, but this mission has to be you."

Bishop nodded. Paul was right, though he wished he wasn't. Bishop had never refused his boss, not once. This was the closest he had ever been to saying no to the man.

"How did you two meet?" Paul's casual tone was forced. "I don't believe you ever told me."

"Didn't I?" Bishop knew he was being interrogated. "It was back in my SAS days. I was young and indestructible. I was at Hereford, in a boxing match, outclassed by some meathead two divisions above me with a personal vendetta. I noticed Argento in the crowd—in a sea of uniforms he was the only one in a suit. I was getting the absolute bejesus smacked out of me. You ever boxed?"

"Can't say I have, no."

"It's not like you see in the movies. It's brutal. I was getting pummelled, the guy was using me as a sandbag. By the fourth round I was having trouble keeping my gloves up. Didn't even see the left hook coming. Knocked me off my feet and I was face down. I can still see Kevin's —I mean, Argento's face. He leaned into the ring and said, 'You should stay down, son.'"

"They were his first words to you?"

"Yeah. 'You should stay down, son.' Like I said, I was young and indestructible. I pushed myself up, wiped the blood with my glove and went back at it. I ended up knocking the other guy out in the fifth. Argento later said it was the damnedest thing he'd ever seen."

Paul hardly blinked. "Why was he there?"

"Recruiting. He was ex-SAS and had a project to bring more SAS-trained personnel into MI6. I was his first protégé."

Paul nodded. "And you built your bond from there."

Bishop smirked at Paul's less than subtle probing. "Correct." Bishop paused. "But we didn't part on the best terms. Because of…" He didn't need to say Tessa's name. "I'm not exactly one of his favourite people. When he found out I was dating his daughter he resigned rather than risk coming across me accidentally. I doubt he'd even talk to me."

"Talking isn't exactly high on the agenda here."

It was an odd choice of words, Bishop thought, and it put him even more on edge. He decided to address it directly, dreading the reply. "So, I'm to capture him? Extract him through, I'm guessing, Hong Kong?"

Paul held his gaze. "No. MI6 and the minister believe he's far too dangerous. He needs to be taken out. There will be no extraction. This is a wet job, pure and simple."

The room spun. Bishop had to hunt down the man who had mentored him, the father of the woman he had loved more than anyone he'd ever known, and kill him? How could he live with that? How could he do it to Tessa? The very thought made him ill. Bishop had to make a choice: eliminate his old mentor or allow him to start a war. The man had saved his life, had given him a new one.

"Paul, I'm going to be honest. This isn't sitting right. Not at all. It doesn't even make sense. This goes against everything the man ever stood for."

Paul nodded and peered through the window to the

slow-moving Thames outside. "He doesn't particularly like the Chinese, does he?"

"After what happened to Ashley, can you blame him?"

"That was a GPS error—not exactly the fault of the Chinese."

"That's what they say." Bishop followed Paul's gaze out the window.

Ashley was Tessa's brother. Like his father, Ashley had joined the Royal Navy. He'd sworn he had no intention of applying for the SAS, having grown up in Hereford and resenting it. He'd stuck to his word and was a ten-year Navy veteran. He'd been on a routine patrol of the South China Sea aboard the *HMS Albion* when it had apparently strayed into Chinese territory. The official account stated that it was a GPS error on the British side. Regardless of the cause, the two sides had engaged in increasingly hostile threats resulting in an exchange of fire. The *Albion* was hit by an air-to-surface missile from a Chinese J-20 fighter. Thirty-two lives were lost, including Ashley's. The Chinese had helped rescue survivors, but the damage had been done.

The resulting inquest cleared the Chinese of blame, as the Albion had strayed into Chinese territorial waters. Kevin had attended every day of the inquest. Bishop went to the reading of the findings, but Argento had refused to shake Bishop's hand, or even to speak to him. Unlike his daughter. The two had broken up before the incident, but the moment Tessa saw Bishop at the inquest she'd launched herself into his arms. Bishop had gone to show his support for both of them, but only one Argento was interested.

Paul sniffed. "You think this could be some kind of revenge spree? For what happened to his son?"

Like many times before, Paul seemed to be reading his mind. "I suppose it's possible. Academically, at least."

"But you don't think so?"

Bishop shook his head. "I know the man—well, I used to. He's not one to run off and kill indiscriminately. He knows what the consequences of his actions would be. The man fought for his country vehemently, put his life on the line countless times to protect her. It doesn't fit."

"Well, the Home Office thinks it does. That's why you're here."

Bishop frowned. Both men tumbled into their own thoughts for a time. The outside noise of a busy office building encroached the stillness.

"Why a wet job?" Bishop asked, breaking the silence.

"The Minister believes that if we were caught escorting the guilty party from the country it'd be tantamount to collusion. Collusion quickly slides into directives. Directives slips into direct commands and before you know it, we're embroiled in a nuclear war and the Windsor Castle corgis are glowing in the dark."

With a tilt of his head, Bishop acknowledged his boss's statement. He could see the Minister's point. Politically, it would be safer. The worst situation would be if Kevin Argento was captured by the Chinese, put on trial and somehow implicated His Majesty's Government. The ramifications would last decades.

It made sense. It mattered little. Not only was Bishop far from convinced, he was almost certain he was incapable of carrying out the mission.

"Who has he supposedly been taking out?"

"Supposedly?" Paul arched an eyebrow. On receiving no reply, he tapped a few keys on his computer. "First, Zhou Cai, a respected Commander of the Ministry of State Security was found behind the wheel in his driveway with a bullet between his eyes. The engine was still running. Second, Yao Qing, a cultural attaché normally assigned to the UN in New York and prior to that, the embassy in Canada, was found in a Tangshan hotel lift with his throat slit. Both of these were confirmed by our agent embedded in the Chinese Ministry of State Security. When a third was found in his home with a TV cord wrapped around his neck, Chinese intelligence understandably began to, in the vernacular, freak the fuck out."

Bishop nodded. The three deaths were executed differently. For one person to carry out the attacks themselves would have been extremely difficult. Then again, if there was a man alive capable of it, it would be his old mentor. The level of proficiency he'd gained in his time with the Navy, SAS and MI6 meant he was a most formidable weapon.

"You said there was an attempted murder of a politician?"

Paul nodded. "A low-level member of a Defence committee in the National People's Congress was on a visit to a state farm when he was attacked. His security detail was taken out and the minister was shot twice in the chest and a bullet grazed his skull. How he survived, I have no idea."

The Mozambique Drill. A double tap to the torso and one bullet to the head just to be sure. Bishop knew the technique well. Kevin Argento had taught him. The more Bishop heard, the more it sounded like his old mentor, and yet, there was a feeling deep within him that it was impossible, that it didn't fit.

"How do you know it's Kevin? I mean, are we sure? It could be a team of—"

His words were cut short when Paul swivelled his computer monitor. "Taken by a member of the Minister's support team."

The image was relatively clean; slightly blurry, but clear enough. The background was rice paddies and blue sky. In the foreground, a figure wore a black jacket and a white, blood splattered shirt. He was running from a crumpled figure on the ground behind him. His face was more wrinkled than Bishop remembered, and there were more grey hairs, but one thing was certain: it was Kevin Argento.

Bishop stared at the image for a long time and Paul let him. In the agent's mind, if he could find some anomaly, some problem with the image, he could out it as a forgery.

As if reading his mind again, Paul said, "The boffins have been over it for hours. As certain as we can be about these things, the photo is genuine." He sighed heavily. "Right now, the Chinese government don't know who he is. If they find out, well…"

Paul didn't need to finish. The two spies knew it wouldn't end well; the sentence or the crisis. Bishop felt increasingly like he was being backed into a corner. The wave of encroaching dread became a tsunami.

"Wait." Bishop sat up. "You're sure the Chinese government doesn't know who Argento is?"

Paul shrugged. "As far as we know. We have people in their intelligence community, law enforcement and military forces, none have come up with any flags on—"

"Then how do you explain the goons that were after Tessa?"

Leaning back, Paul's fingers drummed on his desk. "I… I can't. Nor do I believe in coincidences. Either there's something else at play or someone in the Chinese government has suppressed Argento's identity. Either of those scenarios means we need you on a plane ASAP."

Bishop's mind was racing. "Why was a member of a defence committee visiting a farm?"

Paul frowned, then shook his head. "I don't know, nor do I need to. What I *do* know is that an ex-MI6 agent is killing foreign nationals on their home soil and needs to be stopped. As soon as the Chinese catch him this thing will turn into a shooting war faster than you can say 'nuclear fallout'." Paul theatrically hit a key on his keyboard. "I've sent you the mission dossier. Everything you need is in there." He paused, regarding Bishop. "We can't offer you a lot of support. Sending in more agents will just add legitimacy to any belief this was a sanctioned deployment. We'll support you where we can, but your resources will be limited, I'm afraid."

Bishop nodded. "And our agent in the Ministry of State Security?"

"Has gone silent."

"Oh, marvellous."

Leaning over his desk, Paul used the intercom to request two teas. They arrived alarmingly quickly. Sitting and sipping their drinks, the two relaxed slightly.

"I'm sorry it has to be you, Charles. It's a bastard of an assignment."

Stirring his tea, Bishop offered no reply, lost in thought.

Paul stared into his cup. "Just what do you think he's going to do when he sees you?"

Bishop inhaled deeply. "The man who not only has years of specialised tactical training, but taught classes on it? The soldier who literally wrote the book on infiltration techniques? The man who could take out a target at a distance of over a kilometre with a smashed sniper scope —that man?" Bishop sighed and peered out the window. "I imagine we'll have a pleasant cup of tea."

"Quite." Paul seemed to regret asking, but went on. "Do you remember him well? What he was like back then?"

Bishop eyed his superior suspiciously. As casual as the question sounded, he knew his superior was still testing him. "Oh, yeah, sure. I remember everything about him, you always do with a mentor. Then things turned... but it was different times, we were different people." Bishop paused. "I was even known by a different name."

Paul knew the story too. Charles Bishop hadn't always existed. He'd been invented. The Doctor Frankenstein who had created that particular monster was the reason the two men sat across from each other now. The man responsible for giving Charles Bishop his name was Kevin Argento.

When he was a teen—before he started to get into trouble—Bishop had discovered his love for people-watching. Whenever he had the chance he'd head down to the Leeds railway station and watch the passing public for hours on end. There would be people scurrying off to work, family reunions, breakups, flirtations, aggravations. A microcosm of humanity all in one place. The young Bishop was fascinated. It was exhilarating and confusing all at once.

Now, watching the concourse of Heathrow from the first-class lounge, he observed humanity just as he used to, but with a different eye. A far more cynical eye. Every stranger could be an enemy. Every passer-by may very well wish him or others harm. He assessed every individual as a threat and mused how he'd take each of them down. Bishop had come a long way since those teenage years. He wasn't entirely sure he was happy with the end result.

As he sipped his whiskey sour his thoughts turned

towards more recent events. Seeing Tessa had dredged up feelings he'd long since buried. The confusing and contradictory stories about her father made it impossible for Bishop to land on one emotional state. Everything was churned up and mixed in together. He wasn't sure if the answer lay at the bottom of the glass, but he was determined to find out.

After their confrontation with the would-be interrogators and police, Bishop had spent time with Tessa. It was confusing. He still cared for her, but they weren't in love. So what was she? Attempting to recapture the cynicism with which he'd been watching the airport passers-by, Bishop attempted to place Tessa in an indifferent category, far away from the emotions he'd once felt. It didn't work. Time hadn't erased what he'd felt, and nor had the conquests he'd had since she left.

There was a reason he'd chosen not to contact Tessa since seeing her the day before. Try as he might, the hardened sardonic persona he'd so carefully cultured crumbled around her. There was no way he would allow that to affect his mission. He could have called her, but he knew it would be a mistake. This mission would be hard enough without the guilt of lying to her. And lie he would. How could he tell the woman he used to love that her father, his past mentor, was a murderous aggressor hellbent on shoving the world over the precipice of war? Worse, how could he ever look her in the eye knowing he was the one who had slain the man she'd idolised since birth?

No. He would never contact Tessa again. It was cold and it was heartless, but Bishop would have to get used to the sentiment sooner rather than later. His emotionless assessment of the passengers was part of him readying himself for the callousness to come. There were many within MI6 who viewed him as a blunt instrument;

unthinking and ruthless. That's exactly what he'd need to become to succeed in this mission.

He sipped his drink and sunk deeper into his malaise. Wiggling his glass at the barman, he requested another. It was the only way he'd sleep on the way over. Guilt had a way of keeping one's mind active.

Checking the departures board, Bishop calculated how many drinks he could fit in before the flight to Beijing. It was a lot. He'd need every one of them.

"Remember the time we got stinking drunk in Rome?"

At first Bishop ignored the comment, believing it was part of the background chatter of the airport lounge, but the familiarity of the voice made him snap back to attention. That voice. *The* voice. He turned.

"I threw up in the Trevi Fountain and we both fell asleep on the Spanish Steps." Her smile was wide, but the humour didn't reach her eyes. "This is the second time I've seen you drunk in two days." She shrugged. "I do hope you haven't become a drunk since I've been gone. It's such a cliché."

"Tessa, what… what are you doing here?"

"Getting something to drink." She held up a highball glass with clear liquid and a slice of lemon. "G&T." She took a sip. "Lovely. It better be, it cost more than my first car."

"I don't understand."

"I bought it from some guy down the pub, said he would give me the keys for four pints and a packet of crisps. Salt and vinegar if I remember correctly. Terrible deal, the bloody thing only lasted a few weeks before it blew a head gasket."

"No." Bishop sat up with a sigh. "I mean, why are you here, at the airport?"

"What can I say? I'm a girl who loves to travel."

Bishop rubbed his temples. "Smug doesn't suit you."

Tessa beamed at him. She seemed rather pleased with herself. "No?" Beside her was a cabin baggage-sized suitcase. "Well, avoiding me doesn't suit you."

"Avoiding you is exactly what people do when they break up. It's a well-known fact."

"Is it now?"

"Apparently so."

"Well I'll be." Tessa sipped her drink and glared at him. "Do you know where he is?"

"I have a question of my own. Why are you here, Tessa? Wait, before that, how are you here? How did you know I was going to be at the airport?"

For a moment, there was a coy expression on her face, which soon morphed into self-satisfaction. Eventually she settled on pleased with herself. "Your pot plants."

Bishop blinked several times. "I have to say, that's not the answer I was expecting."

"You haven't changed, Charles. Whenever you went on missions you slipped the doorman a few pounds to water your plants while you were gone." She shrugged. "He texted me this morning to say you were going away, and, well, here I am."

"Remind me to have Brian fired, will you?"

"I don't think I will, no." She squinted. "You're going to China to find Dad, aren't you?"

"What makes you think I'm going to China?"

Tessa glanced down. "Your boarding pass, for one."

She was right, his boarding pass clearly listed Beijing as the destination.

"Quite the detective." Bishop sighed. "That's just the first leg. I'm really off to Greenland." Seeing the scepticism on her face, he added, "I have a really terrible travel agent."

"Stop being a twat." She slapped her own boarding pass on top of his. "I'm coming too."

He shouldn't have been surprised. Tessa had always been smart, smarter than him. He should have taken that into account. Now she was here in front of him, he may as well ask her something that had been playing on his mind.

"Tessa, your father…" Bishop paused, trying to select the right words. "How's he been since Ashley passed?"

Curiosity crossed her features before she drifted into thoughtfulness. "Okay, I guess, as well as…" She paused and held his gaze. "No, that's the usual response. Not good, Charles. He's become increasingly quiet and withdrawn, almost secretive. I thought it might be a new girlfriend he was worried I wouldn't approve of, but no. He's—" she wrung her hands. "I knew it was bigger than that. After those guys stopped me in the street yesterday, I…" Her voice trailed off. "He's in trouble, isn't he?" Receiving no response, she went on. "All the more reason for me to go to China with you."

"Tessa, those blokes on the street were just the start. This goes way beyond what you know. You can't come with me." For a fleeting second their amusement at the inaccuracy of that statement lingered in the air, then Bishop's demeanour turned grave. "It's far too dangerous for you, Tessa."

"Why? Because I'm a woman?"

"No, because you're not a spy. You're not trained for foreign infiltration." Bishop paused. He knew the determined expression on Tessa's face. She wasn't going to be dissuaded. Her determination was one of her defining qualities, one he'd always found attractive. To discourage her, he had to layer what he was saying with elements of truth. Quietly, he went on. "I can't tell you why, but people are dying, Tessa. I'm trying to protect you. Not because you're a woman, but because I don't want you hurt. Sex has nothing to do with it."

"With you, it's always about sex."

Her words were playful but her manner had shifted. His warnings about death and danger had an effect. She was slowly realising this wasn't just about a wayward father. Creases appeared on her forehead, and she glanced off to the side, the way she did when she was mulling things over. While she was distracted, Bishop stood and pulled out his phone.

Turning her attention back to Bishop, Tessa asked, "What do you mean, people are dying?"

Ignoring the question, Bishop held up a finger to say, *hold on a moment*, and texted furiously. Within seconds he sat down again and gestured to a waiter.

Arms steadfastly crossed, Tessa scowled. "I asked you a question."

Nodding in her direction, Bishop turned to the newly arrived waiter and carefully ordered the most complicated cocktail he could. All the while, Tessa seethed.

Once he had finished, Bishop turned and asked, "Where were we?"

"You know perfectly bloody well. What do you mean—"

"Attention, passengers." The announcement echoed from the speakers.

"We'd better listen." Bishop pointed up. "Might be important."

"Could Ms Tessa Argento flying to Beijing aboard British Airways please report to the service desk. Repeat, could Ms Tessa Argento please report to the service desk, thank you."

"Well," Bishop said, pure as virgin driven snow, "it was indeed important after all."

Eyes narrowing, Tessa growled. "What have you done?"

A splayed hand to his chest, Bishop opened his mouth in mock shock and mouthed, *me?*

Tessa stormed off to the service desk. From where he sat, Bishop could see her hand gestures grow wilder and the aggravation on her face increase exponentially. Over the next few minutes, anger gave way to acceptance and her shoulders slumped. Eventually she turned and thundered towards Bishop.

"You added me to the fucking no-fly list, you bastard."

"You're on the no-fly list? Really? There must be some sort of mistake, surely. Let's get to the bottom of this. Oh, wait." Bishop glanced at his watch, barely long enough to register the time. "Damn, I have a flight to catch. Such a shame." He picked up his cabin bag. "I do hope you get the misunderstanding sorted. All the best."

Collapsing in her seat, Tessa shook her head. "I won't forget this, you know." She frowned, but Bishop detected the faintest of smirks, as if she was mildly impressed at being outmanoeuvred.

He knew perfectly well she'd never forget it, just as he knew he couldn't allow Tessa to fly into a hostile environment. If the Chinese were bold enough to confront her on the street in her own country, there was be no way she would be afforded restraint on their home soil. No, for Tessa to remain safe she had to remain in the UK. This mission was tough enough already without having to worry about Tessa. Bishop was a professional who had yet to fail in an assignment. He had never strayed from mission parameters, but he knew if she was in danger his allegiance could very well be challenged, no matter what the stakes were. It was a risk he couldn't afford to take.

As he left the lounge, he turned to see the dirty look

smeared across Tessa's face. She most likely hated his very soul at that moment in time. It was something Bishop could live with if it meant keeping her grounded. Keeping her safe.

He made his way to the gate and was ushered through to first class. The middle-aged flight attendant had a pleasant smile. "May I hang your jacket, sir?" Bishop nodded and handed it to her. As she hung it, she asked, "Business or pleasure?"

Bishop didn't have to spend any time considering his answer.

"Business." His tone was firm.

She nodded and went to attend to the next passenger. Bishop slumped into his seat. His trip was pure business. That was the only way to classify travelling halfway around the world to murder a friend.

CHAPTER THREE

"Looks heavy."

Bishop turned to see a well-dressed Asian woman standing beside him at the baggage carousel. She wore a black well-tailored business suit, equally black turtleneck and had silky long straight hair. He didn't recall seeing her on his flight, and he would have definitely remembered her. Her strong angular face was softened by her stunning green eyes. She wouldn't have been out of place on a catwalk. Her English was perfectly enunciated.

"This old thing? Light as a feather." Bishop hefted the bag from the carousel and grunted in exertion as he did so. They both chuckled at his failed attempt at machismo.

It was indeed heavy. MI6 had a baggage handler on the payroll at the Beijing airport who, when required, would slip in an extra case to supply operatives with weapons and surveillance equipment. They had another in the customs queue. It eliminated all the fuss of being hauled into immigration and executed as a spy. Quite handy.

The woman continued to stare at Bishop with her stunning eyes, a knowing smirk dancing on her lips.

When Bishop collected his other bag, the one he had legitimately checked in at Heathrow, the woman stayed by his side. Not engaging in further chitchat, Bishop followed the signs to immigration. The green-eyed woman kept pace, occasionally throwing him a knowing grin. She had no baggage with her, apart from a large black handbag.

When the long line of customs loomed ahead she peeled off and was lost in the crowd. Part of Bishop wanted to dismiss their meeting as a case of mistaken identity. But the spy in him knew he could never afford such luxury.

The progress through immigration was efficient. Following instructions, he chose the leftmost queue and was processed without incident or acknowledgement. MI6's man in the customs uniform passed him through like he would any other passenger. Soon Bishop was through, and officially in China. He followed the signs to the taxi rank. The throng was around twenty people deep, the wait not too long.

As he waited, Bishop mentally prepared himself for what was to come. Or at least tried to. This was his most personal mission, not one he relished, and one he would do his best to purge from his memory when it was done.

At an academic level, Bishop understood why he'd been tapped on the shoulder for the mission. He did know Argento better than anyone. His mentor had made him into a good soldier and an even better spy. He'd shown Bishop all his tricks, his techniques, his methodologies and countermeasures to all of them. Argento had turned Bishop into the perfect spy. And now that spy was going to hunt him down.

Being the professional that he was, Bishop accepted every mission with enthusiasm, but never bloodthirsty zeal. The personal nature of this assignment was so foreign to him it was almost impossible to comprehend. The man he had revered as a second father was now the enemy. And given the success rate of Bishop's missions, he would soon be dead. He wondered if he'd be able to look at himself in the mirror ever again.

Before he could slide deeper into the disquiet that had plagued him on the flight over, Bishop sensed a presence beside him. He tilted his head and saw who it was.

He sighed. "Do we know each other?"

The woman with the green eyes smiled. "Not yet." She raised a seductive eyebrow.

Bishop decided the time for polite chitchat was over. "I assume you work for someone. Care to tell me who?"

"Also," she dazzled him with a toothy grin, "not yet."

Mind racing, Bishop sized up his new shadow. If she were immigration or State Security he wouldn't have been allowed into the country. They would have seized him as soon as he touched down. So who the hell was she?

The airport was crowded. Hundreds of people piled in and out every few seconds. Travellers streamed between floors and from section to section. If he chose to, he could return to the terminal, immerse himself in the crowd and lose his eager young escort. About to do exactly that, Bishop noticed three men dressed in dark suits, glaring at him. They whispered among themselves, and the eldest, who had a distinctive purple birthmark across the right side of his face, jabbed his fingers, directing them to either side of where Bishop stood.

The green-eyed woman didn't take her eyes off the new arrivals. "You've got company."

"Seems I do."

"What are you going to do about it?"

Bishop watched as all three men approached from

different vectors. "Do I have enough time to buy a pantomime horse outfit?"

The woman tore her gaze from the encroaching men and stared at Bishop as if he was the stupidest man alive. It was entirely possible that he was.

With five people ahead of him in the taxi line, Bishop estimated that the men would intercept him before he reached the front.

The green-eyed woman tugged at his sleeve. "I have a car not far from here."

"My mother always told me not to get into cars with strangers."

Her words urgent, the green-eyed woman lowered her voice. "Did she say anything about avoiding the Ministry of State Security?"

That was interesting. She knew that the men worked for the equivalent of MI6. *Who the hell is she?*

"Oh, plenty. She gave me a watch with a garrotte wire for my third birthday."

She smiled. "That was quick. Good job."

"Why thank you." Bishop eyed the lead man; he was going to intercept them first.

"State Security don't appreciate funny. Your humour will be lost on them."

"Oh, I don't know. I have some Mao knock knock jokes that'll slay them."

Were they who she said they were? Again, Bishop came back to the same question: *Why didn't they stop me at customs?* If they thought he was a threat, there was a simple way to stop him from messing up their country: don't let him in. If they were actually Ministry of State Security they wouldn't take kindly to a spy's presence, nor to the weapons and surveillance equipment in his suitcase. He couldn't take the risk. Bishop had to move.

Taxis in Beijing all had a yellow stripe. Whether the

car was red, white or blue, they all had the same stripe. Picking up his bags, Bishop rushed forward, past the handful of passengers patiently waiting their turn.

The taxi driver was out of his still-running vehicle, cigarette dangling from his bottom lip. Pushing a couple in business suits aside, Bishop heaved his bags into the boot and rounded the driver's side of the car. It took a moment for the passengers and driver to comprehend what had just happened, but soon a torrent of angry Mandarin was hurled Bishop's way. The verbal assault increased when the other passengers in line joined in. Ignoring them all, Bishop jumped in behind the wheel and slammed the door shut.

As Bishop slid the car into the gear, the passenger side door was flung open and the green-eyed woman leapt in. With zero seconds to decide what to do and the taxi driver, nearby police and the suited heavies all zeroing in, Bishop floored it. Tyres screeched as the taxi took off, leaving everyone in their wake.

Thirty metres up the road, Bishop slammed on the brakes. The woman beside him slammed into the dash, not having managed to put on her seatbelt. For a moment, the taxi driver must have thought he was getting his vehicle back. But it wasn't to be. The sudden stop slammed the boot shut, and then Bishop took off again at speed.

Within half a minute Bishop had merged with the hundreds of other taxis squeezing through the multiple exits of the Beijing Capital International Airport. They were soon lost in the sea of taxis.

"You're certainly unexpected." The woman beside him beamed as she clicked in her seatbelt. "I'll give you that."

"You're certainly persistent, I'll give you *that*." Bishop smiled back. "And if you don't tell me who the fuck you are in five seconds, I'm throwing you out of this car. No more coy bullshit."

"Direct." Her eyes had fire in them. "I like it."

Bishop swerved around a slow-moving taxi. The merging traffic appeared like a giant throng of bugs crawling over one another, morphing, expanding and contracting en masse. No one honked, no one seemed to get angry. This was how traffic was in Beijing.

Without taking his eyes off the chaos before him, Bishop unclicked the green-eyed woman's seatbelt and let it retract. "Now."

"Fine," she said, folding her arms. "I'm from the Service's Hong Kong office. Zhao Chen. '6 thought you could use some support. Someone who could, ah, blend in a little better, shall we say?"

Bishop growled. "You could have said that at the start." He turned to her and saw a fleeting smirk.

"I wanted to get the measure of you."

The tension eased. A fellow MI6 agent would make sense, given the magnitude of the mission. With no obvious tail, Bishop relaxed, but only slightly.

"I assure you, good woman, if you wanted my measure, all you had to do was ask." Bishop cast his best rogue grin, then his expression turned more serious. "I don't need a babysitter."

"Vauxhall Cross thinks otherwise. Given your escapades in Haiti, they thought it best you work with a partner for a change."

"I had a partner in Haiti. Of sorts."

She tilted her head. "And didn't that work out well?"

Only someone from MI6 would have that knowledge. She was indeed a fellow agent. Her presence complicated matters—he'd been planning on a solo mission—but in many respects would likely aid his investigations. That didn't mean he trusted her yet, though. Bishop remapped his thinking as he drove.

"What do I call you, Zhao?"

She sighed. "The Chinese state their last name first, followed by the given name. For example, Liu Jianguo, in Chinese would be Mr Jianguo Liu using the Western style. Never call someone by only his or her first name."

"Understood, Zhao."

Raising a finger to argue the point, she sighed and slumped back in her seat. "Can I put my seatbelt back on now?" Bishop nodded.

"Can we stop for a burger or something? I'm starving." Zhao had an expectant expression.

"We don't have time," Bishop said flatly.

"Oh, we're not going to get along at all then. Eating's kind of my thing."

Scanning the traffic, Bishop didn't reply. Now that she'd put the idea in his head, he was kind of peckish, but couldn't very well stop when he was driving a stolen taxi.

Apparently needing to fill the silence, Zhao spoke again. "Do you have an actual plan or are you just going to steal stuff and cause chaos across China?"

Bishop picked a gap between two lorries and found the traffic speeding up finally. "Were those guys back there really Ministry of State Security?"

"Can't be one hundred per cent, but reasonably sure."

He had gone to an awful amount of effort if they were just pushy limo drivers, Bishop mused. No, they had to be after him directly, and the only reasonable conclusion was State Security. But that didn't answer all of it. "Why did they let me outside the airport if they suspected I was a spy?"

Zhao shrugged. "The Chinese are naturally suspicious people. That goes for foreigners, but also their own government institutions. The police don't trust the army. Party officials don't trust business leaders. Nobody trusts the Ministry of State Security." She eyed a slow-moving Mercedes that had been keeping pace with them for thirty seconds. When it peeled away, she went on. "The Ministry probably thought it best to avoid other bureaucracies if they could. Then again, perhaps they just turned up late. Maybe they were after another tall, well-dressed fop. Who knows?"

"Who's a fop?" Bishop frowned.

She was well-versed in Western idioms. Bishop didn't like it.

Zhao peered out her window, examining road signs. "Where are we going?"

"South."

"I can tell that. Anywhere in particular?"

"Yes."

"Are you always this communicative?"

"No."

Zhao folded her arms. "Well, won't this be fun?"

Bishop groaned and silence swirled around them. The traffic chugged and manoeuvred in the dying light of the day. The sound of the tyres hitting the road reverberated through the car.

"Been in this game long?" Zhao's tone was softer.

Bishop shrugged. "Long enough to be bitter, not long enough to know why."

"What does that even mean?" Zhao rubbed her eyes. "Want to know anything about me?"

Bishop frowned. "Ever been in the circus?"

Amused, Zhao replied, "No."

"There. I know something about you."

"Fine. If you won't talk to me, I'll do it myself." Sitting back in her seat, she sighed. "So, why did you become a spy, Bishop?" She leaned forward and squinted.

Receiving no reply, she went on. "I'll speculate, shall I? Let's see, I've known you for all of," she checked her watch, "ten minutes now. So, I'm going to say... a woman. Am I close?"

The topic was a little too close to home for him to find her words amusing, so he kept his attention steadfastly on the road before him. Bishop knew he was being difficult. He hadn't confirmed her identity yet, but if she was who she claimed to be, he realised he was being an arsehole. One of his primary skills was charming people, something he seemed utterly incapable of at that precise moment in time. This mission had affected him far more than he realised. It wasn't Zhao's fault, but he wasn't in the mood for playful banter with the newcomer.

"I'll take that masculine silence as a yes then, shall I?" Zhao leaned forward to study his expression, or lack thereof. "Excellent, now we're getting somewhere. But it couldn't be as straightforward as a jilted love affair." She tilted her head. "No, too pedestrian. You had a torrid affair with the headmaster's wife and absconded with the fete funds. Or maybe you ran up a tab with all the bookies in London, and it was either be a spy or join the French Foreign Legion. No, wait, I have it. You killed a mime."

Bishop frowned. "Well, if you must know, I joined MI6 for the short hours, free jet skis and generous pension."

"Yeah, we don't have any of those things."

"Really? I must have been misinformed."

Zhao shook her head. "Are you always this charming?"

"You should see me when I'm surly."

"I'm finding it hard to imagine what that's like. Nope, absolutely no idea."

Folding her arms, Zhao lapsed into silence. After a few minutes Bishop sensed he was under surveillance.

"Why are you staring?" He glanced at Zhao, who was indeed watching him.

"My handler didn't mention how handsome you were."

"Really? That's so odd. That's usually in the mission briefing. Sex, height, weight, hair colour, rating on Hot or Not."

"And you can be funny when you're not being an arse." She gave a mischievous grin.

"If we're to be working together—"

"Closely, I hope," she positively purred.

"As I said, working together, there's one thing you must know about me."

Zhao raised an eyebrow. "And that is?"

"I don't play well with others."

Giving Bishop a smirk, Zhao wrinkled her nose. "Oh, I find that very difficult to believe."

The two fell into silence, immersed in their own thoughts. Bishop wondered if Zhao's were as creative as his.

For the next half hour Bishop weaved through Beijing's chaotic traffic, keeping an eye on any vehicle that lingered in his rear-view mirror for more than a minute. They had no tail.

He'd insisted on taking a photo of Zhao and sending it through to MI6 to confirm her identity. Within minutes, MI6 sent back a text confirming she was who she claimed to be. Zhao issued Bishop a smug expression that lasted a good ten minutes. It didn't make Bishop any less resentful about being issued a babysitter.

Approaching his destination, Bishop left the highway and wove through the winding local streets. Hundreds of overhead electrical wires crisscrossed above dirty, garbage-filled streets.

"Xinjian Village?" Zhao asked in surprise. "Why on earth are we here?"

"I never visit a city without knowing where the sleaziest parts are."

Zhao turned to him. "There are just so many ways I could take that statement."

As he searched for a place to park, Bishop explained. "Taxis have GPS trackers. Sooner or later they're going to start looking for us." Bishop paused as he slid the car into an available slot on a quiet side street. "We'll be long gone by then." He turned off the engine, leaving the keys in the ignition, then pressed the boot release and exited. Zhao followed him to the rear of the vehicle. "Whoever was after me at the airport will be chasing their tails all day and we'll be long gone."

Zhao harrumphed. "Yeah. A six-foot, blond, blue-eyed dude totally won't stand out in a Beijing crowd."

"Ah, but you're forgetting one thing." From his suitcase, Bishop extracted a grey peaked cap, mirrored sunglasses and a different jacket. "I'm a master of disguise."

Zhao rolled her eyes. Bishop put on his disguise. He also armed himself with two pistols from his MI6-issued weapons pack. He didn't offer anything to Zhao, for two reasons. One, he assumed she was already armed. Two, he'd confirmed her identity, but that didn't mean he trusted her yet. In the espionage business, blind trust got you killed.

As they walked away from the taxi, two dishevelled locals leaning against a graffiti-stained wall eyed Bishop and Zhao hungrily. Doubling back, Bishop opened the driver's side door and pulled out the keys. He tossed them to one of the men, giving him a nod.

As they rounded the corner, Zhao glanced back at the two men approaching the taxi, but said nothing. After a minute of walking, she finally asked, "Where to now?"

Seeing the sign for the underground train station, Bishop sped up. "We go see The Pope."

Zhao stopped walking and her mouth dropped open as she gawped at him. "I can't say that's the answer I expected."

CHAPTER FOUR

Two underground lines and five changes of direction later, they arrived at their destination: a once-palatial missionary mansion on the outskirts of the Changyingxiang district. Likely built in the twenties, the grand old building may have been impressive once, but the windows were boarded up and it was in a state of disrepair. *The Pollard Mission* was carved in large letters over the huge double doors. Bishop considered it the height of imperial arrogance that the building's name was emblazoned in English.

It was set among a forested park that backed onto a golf club. The rest of the neighbourhood buildings were upmarket and modern, in direct contrast to the once stately old ministry. It seemed nobody had the heart to knock it down. Night was falling, and the dark purple sky framed the old sandstone mission, giving it a majestic hue, even in its decaying state.

Having stowed their bags at the local train station, Bishop walked unencumbered up the worn stairwell leading to the huge weathered wooden doors. Zhao followed.

"I saw a KFC back there." She gestured behind them. "We could…"

"We ate at the station." Bishop's voice was hushed.

"That was a light snack at best."

Bishop stopped climbing and turned. "Are you perpetually hungry?"

"Not always, no."

"No?"

"No." Zhao gave him a slanted grin. "Sometimes I'm asleep."

With a shake of his head, Bishop continued ascending the stairs. When he reached the entrance, Bishop rapped the old iron knocker several times, then stepped back.

"Are you sure anyone lives here?" Zhao frowned. "It seems abandoned."

"Looks can be deceiving." Bishop raised an eyebrow and paused in anticipation, then sighed. "Damn it. That would have been perfect if the door had opened. Now the moment's ruined." He used the heavy door knocker once more, the sound reverberating into the still night air. Pressing his face to the space where the two doors met, Bishop yelled, "It's Bishop. Open up, you old coot!"

For several seconds, nothing happened. Then there was shuffling behind the door and the clicks of locks being undone. The door was heaved open to reveal an African American man in his late fifties with a receding hairline and a pot belly. Despite having been embedded in China for years, he still dressed like an American: jeans, polo and sneakers.

When his tired eyes met Bishop's, he sighed. "You here to kill me?"

"No," Bishop replied evenly. "I'm here for information."

The man grunted. "With you could be one and the same." He turned Zhao. "Who's the chick?"

"MI6 too. Zhao Chen."

The man rolled his eyes. "Fucken spies." He opened the door wider. "Best come in then. Don't think I have much choice anyway."

The Pope was ex-NSA. He'd been stationed in China for twenty years, retired for five. He and Bishop had first crossed paths when The Pope had been seconded in London, tasked with sharing Chinese counter-surveillance techniques with his cousins across the pond. When they'd met, Bishop could tell The Pope's heart still belonged back east. He'd retired soon after, and moved to China permanently. Both CIA and MI6 had attempted to recruit him, even on a part-time basis, but he'd refused all offers—sometimes robustly. Bishop hadn't been sure The Pope would even open the door for him.

The two MI6 spies crossed the threshold into what had once been a grand entrance but had fallen on hard times. The faded walls had chunks of plaster missing, and clearly hadn't seen a paintbrush in a hundred years. The black and white floor tiles were carved with age and dirt. The whole place dripped with decay and neglect.

At the end of the hall they followed The Pope down a short flight of stairs, to what appeared to be a basement. Their host pressed a notch of wood on the frame of an old tattered tapestry and the tapestry slid silently sideways, into the wall beside it. The room behind the tapestry was like nothing in the hallway. Stark white and modernist, the brightly lit space wouldn't have been out of place in a lavish New York apartment. It was a huge open-plan living area, containing a lounge, dining and kitchen. The furniture was a mix of expensive antiques and luxurious modern furnishings; tasteful, in direct contrast to The Pope's dress sense.

Seeing Zhao's astonished expression, The Pope grinned and gestured to the filthy hallway behind them.

"For outsiders." He turned to Bishop, assessing him with disdain. "Façades can be deceptive. Ain't that right, pretty boy?"

Stepping into the luxuriously appointed apartment, Bishop slapped his host on the shoulder. "Got any scotch?"

The Pope beckoned to Zhao, inviting her into his lair. She nodded her thanks.

"I have bourbon." The Pope strode towards an antique art nouveau drinks cabinet. "Or bourbon."

"My, what a choice." Bishop smirked. "Bourbon, thank you."

When The Pope turned to Zhao she shook her head. "Thank you, no." She looked at Bishop. "I'm on duty."

The Pope and Bishop exchanged looks and smirked. Chuckling to himself, The Pope poured two bourbons—neat—and handed one to Bishop.

"What's this about, pretty boy?"

"You already know." Bishop took a sip. Smooth, expensive. Not to his tastes, but it would do. "Or you wouldn't have let me in. Do you know where he is?"

Shaking his head, The Pope frowned. "Been out of the business for years, man."

Bishop did his best not to roll his eyes. "Can we skip the bit where you deny and I ask you several times over? It's tedious, I don't have time and I have a serious case of jet lag, so if we could just..." Bishop rolled his hand in a *speed it up* motion.

The Pope shrugged. "My little mice have heard rumours, whispers in the wind." He took a large swig and slammed the glass down, then raised an eyebrow, challenging Bishop to finish his own. When Bishop complied, The Pope refilled their glasses and went on. "I'm not surprised they sent you. You know him best. You're probably the only one who could talk him out of whatever madness he's under." The Pope handed Bishop his glass but didn't relinquish his hold on it. He studied Bishop's face intently and tilted his head. "But you're not here to talk to him, are you?"

"Where is he?"

"You didn't answer my question."

Bishop sneered. "You didn't answer mine."

The Pope nodded and let go of the glass, and the two men eyed one another coolly. As Zhao opened her mouth to break the uneasy silence, a door opened on the other side of the open plan living area. A short Asian woman in her late thirties entered carrying two grocery bags. On seeing Bishop and Zhao, she let out a small shriek.

Palms up, The Pope approached and spoke in hushed Mandarin. The delicacy of his tone and the gentle kiss on the cheek told Bishop this was his partner. She soon calmed, and nodded a careful hello to the two strangers.

The Pope stepped forward. "My wife, Ying Yue."

Bishop stepped forward and extended a hand. "Xiè xie nǐ. Nǐ yǒu yīgè kě'ài de jiā."

They all regarded him with astonished expressions as he thanked Ying Yue for welcoming them into her home. Zhao's eyes were the widest.

"Very nice words, thank you." Ying Yue grinned. "But your pronunciation is atrocious."

Zhao shook her head in agreement. "So bad."

The Pope made quick introductions. Ying Yue greeted them both warmly. She didn't ask why they were there or how they knew her husband. She must have known enough about his former profession to understand there were questions you never ask.

Ying Yue rounded the kitchen bench and unpacked the groceries. "You're staying for dinner, of course?"

Zhao virtually jumped up and down in excitement, but remained mute. The ex-NSA agent gave Bishop the slightest shake of his head. Bishop acknowledged the signal with a nod, then turned and bowed to Ying Yue. "That would be lovely. I'm quite famished. Thank you."

The Pope grunted.

Bishop leaned back, sated, and placed his chopsticks beside his plate. The Pope was the only one who ate with a fork. He'd claimed he could use chopsticks, but not at a pace a man of his size could subsist on. Bishop didn't buy it, and suspected he clung to his Westerner ways as a last bastion of his past life.

"That was utterly delicious, thank you, Ying Yue."

She grinned and collected the plates. "You're welcome. Not bad for an archaeology professor, hey?"

Taking the plates to the kitchen, she left them alone.

Zhao watched her go, then turned to her host. "How long have you lived in China, ah—do I call you The Pope, Mr Pope?"

"Lawrence is fine." He smiled politely. "Over twenty years. Came here in the nineties attached to the embassy, when they couldn't keep up with the leaps the Chinese were making in communications technology. Managed to keep finding excuses to stay." His eyes grew thoughtful. "I fell in love with the country. Some parts more than others," he added, eyeing his wife stacking the dishwasher.

Bishop followed his gaze. "She's lovely. I like her a lot."

"If she loves me even half as much as I love her, then I know I've made her happy. She's an extraordinary woman."

For a moment, Bishop lurched from the present and was reminded of the one love of his life. He wondered if he and Tessa could ever have made it like these two had: doubtful. He also wondered if she'd ever cared for him as passionately as he had once cared for her: possible. Finally, he wondered if she'd stay pissed at him forever for adding her to the no-fly list: undoubtedly.

His wayward thoughts were interrupted by Zhao sitting up with an expectant look on her face. "And how do you two gentlemen know each other?" Zhao's delivery was a little too quick. She'd have to work on her subtlety.

The Pope's eyes narrowed, and his face grew hard. "Like he said, we met in London. But that's not where I got to *know* who he really was. That came later. Your little shit of a partner royally screwed me over."

"Look, if you could possibly overdramatise the story, that would be great." Bishop smirked. Addressing Zhao, he gave his version of the story. Several years before, the UK and US were on a joint mission to apprehend a notorious terrorist recruiter who had been tracked to Macau. It was meant to be a joint collar, but at the last minute Bishop had absconded with the suspect and extradited him to England, allowing the mother country to take credit for the collar.

Zhao screwed up her face. "That seems highly unethical."

Folding his arms, The Pope said, "You're not fucking wrong."

"Oh, come on, the Prime Minister thanked the US." In a lower tone, Bishop added, "Buried deep in the fourth paragraph of the PM's statement. Can't think why he still holds a grudge."

"It seems like a complete mystery." Zhao shook her head.

Bishop went on. "The suspect had information critical to His Majesty's interests which couldn't wait for the

Americans to claim their pound of flesh. We obtained the intelligence and many lives were saved in the process. I'm not going to apologise for that."

The Pope shook his head and poured himself more wine. His body language was less tense now. He wasn't a field agent, and not well-versed at masking his emotions; the truth had clearly lessened his anger. "You could have asked."

"Yes, because the US are normally so generous in their handling of espionage matters."

The Pope tilted his head in acknowledgement. "So, what do you want?"

"I need to find him." Bishop leaned forward. "I know you can help me."

Frowning, The Pope stretched his arms behind his head. "I may have heard a whisper or two." Bishop knew that meant shouts. Understatement was one of The Pope's most annoying traits. He had cultivated a network of informants over his twenty years in the country; that doesn't get turned off overnight.

Bishop waited. Sometimes silence was the best interrogator. The Pope went on. "With the six he's killed, I think—"

"Six?" Silence no longer an option, Bishop sat up. "We've only heard of three, four if you count the politician who survived."

With a frown, The Pope took a swig of his drink. "Seems some of us are better informed than others, eh? Who're yours?"

Bishop paused. The intelligence he had was top secret. The Pope could be playing him, but he doubted it. He weighed up whether to share what he knew.

"This is like a lethal game of Go Fish," Zhao said with a half-smile. Bishop was warming to her.

He sighed. There was no use withholding the information. In order for The Pope to divulge anything, Bishop would need to give up what he had.

"Zhou Cai, Commander of the Ministry of State Security. Yao Qing, a cultural attaché at the UN. A third was found in his home with a TV cord wrapped around his neck. And an unsuccessful attempt on an underling in the Defence committee of the National People's Congress."

With a sage nod, The Pope placed his glass carefully on the table. "He killed a soldier in a field, a kid really, after attempting to assassinate Jiang Huang from the Defence committee. Then there's the latest, just yesterday."

Bishop held his breath. A recent victim would put him within one day's travel. Far closer than any MI6 intelligence placed him.

The Pope went on. "This one was self-defence, it seems. Best my sources can make out, a member of the local police force stumbled on a Western man on a bus acting suspicious. It wasn't until afterwards that the authorities figured out who it was."

"What happened to the police officer?" Zhao's despondent face told Bishop she already suspected what the answer would be.

"Argento shot him in the face and fled. The officer died at the scene."

With a nod, Bishop kept his voice quiet. "Where is he?"

Swirling the liquid in the glass, The Pope stared at it contemplatively. "He's a good man."

"Apart from all the face shooting?" Bishop could hear the emotion he'd allowed to creep into his tone.

The Pope held his gaze. "I don't know what's compelling him to do what he's doing, but you know him. This isn't him. He's better than this. He's a good man."

Bishop didn't move. "I know."

"A good man who's doing some crazy shit."

The MI6 agent's face remained neutral. "I know that too."

"Will you at least talk to him first?"

"I'm not going to promise something I can't—"

The Pope shook his head. "You talk to him first or I give you shit, Bishop. Okay? That's the deal. I'll supply you the means to find him if you promise to talk to him first. Find out why he wants to start World War Three. If he's fucking nuts, fine, put a bullet in him—hell, you can have one of mine." The Pope leaned forward. "But I know the man, and so do you. I'm having a damn hard time believing he's doing all this for shits and giggles. If you're a mile away, watching him through a sniper's scope, you'll never find out. Talk to the man. Look him in the eye. I owe him that. *You* owe him that. That's my price."

Leaning back, Bishop scrutinised the ceiling. He could lie to The Pope and say, "sure, I'll talk to him", and then assassinate him just the same, but that didn't sit right with him. He could see where The Pope was coming from. If the situation was reversed, he'd likely ask the same. Bishop prided himself on being a man of his word. He wouldn't lie to The Pope if he could avoid it.

"Alright. I'll talk to him first." Bishop meant it. If circumstances made it difficult or impossible then he'd have to live with that, but he would do his best to keep his word.

Bishop was just opening his mouth to ask for a location when Ying Yue came running into the room.

"Lawrence, the perimeter alarms have gone off."

The Pope's head snapped around to Bishop, his eyes narrowed, then he rushed to the kitchen and rummaged around in a drawer until he found what he was looking for. He aimed a remote at the TV, which came alive. On screen was grainy night footage, split into four images, different locations exterior to The Pope's mansion. Each image was similar. Black-clad troops wearing balaclavas and tactical webbing, creeping forward with carbine assault weapons.

The Pope turned to Bishop. "You brought this into my house!"

Everyone was on their feet. In the kitchen, The Pope and Ying Yue were engaged in an urgent, hushed discussion.

Zhao leaned over to Bishop and spoke in a hushed tone. "Master of disguise, my skinny arse. They must have tracked you via CCTV in the subway."

Remaining quiet, Bishop assessed the formation of the attackers. They had a minute at best. He turned to The Pope. "I'm genuinely sorry."

"If they make me leave this country because of you I'm hunting you down, Bishop. You understand me?"

He nodded. "I do."

The Pope scrambled to the corner of the open plan room and pushed aside a reading chair. He heaved up a heavy trapdoor.

With one eye on the footage of the encroaching troops, Bishop asked, "What do we do now?"

From the hole in the floor, The Pope threw Bishop a shotgun. "We fight."

CHAPTER FIVE

Arming Zhao and his wife, The Pope closed the trapdoor and slid the chair back into place. Ying Yue held the firearm with such hesitancy Bishop assumed she was inexperienced with firing weapons. Zhao, on the other hand, grasped hers with both hands, checked the balance, counted the shells and cocked the shotgun with confidence.

Dashing to the nearest wall, The Pope pressed some unseen button and a portion of the wall slid silently aside. Behind it, a bank of servers and IT equipment blinked away on racks. Flipping down a protective clear plastic cover, The Pope slapped a large red button on the wall. Instantly the equipment smouldered, smoke billowing from inside the computers.

The Pope pressed a button and the wall slid back in place. He sped away. "Follow me."

Before they reached the other side of the room, the door they had entered through blew off its rails. Four assault troops burst through the chaos of smoke and shouts, with several more taking defensive positions in the hallway. A similar blast behind them, combined with even more shouts, told Bishop they were cut off, outnumbered and outgunned. Beside him, Zhao's grip tightened around the shotgun.

Bishop pushed down the barrel of her gun. "There's no way we win this."

The other two followed his lead and lowered their weapons. The four lead assault troops disarmed them and stood at the centre of the room, a smoke haze swirling around them.

One of the lead assault troops removed his balaclava. Across the right side of his face was a distinctive purple birthmark. The man Bishop had seen at the airport spoke quietly into his lapel mic. Ministry of State Security.

The odds were almost even, but the opposition had the drop. Their weapons were drawn and aimed. No quick draw would succeed. Bishop dropped his shotgun and it clattered to the floor. The others did the same. They couldn't win this one; it was over.

From the original breach door, a tall man appeared. Mid-fifties, he had a severe face that had seemingly developed from a lifetime of scowling. It was a face that conveyed neither warmth nor joy. It was a cruel face.

Stepping forward, he inspected all four, as if assessing their very souls. He didn't appear to like what he saw. The Pope earned a particularly disdainful expression.

The man's expensive black suit and buttoned-up black shirt were expertly tailored. If he was a civil servant, he was a well-paid one. Bishop remained silent.

Taking position in front of Bishop, the newcomer rocked on his heels. "It seems we have a common goal." His English was flawless, with only a hint of an accent. "My name is Chang Yuchin. It seems we have a mutual objective. We have... an opportunity to work together to—"

"You have no right to invade my home like this!"

Chang slapped The Pope across the face. It was a decent backhander, delivered with force. To his credit, the big man staggered only slightly, but more importantly made no move to retaliate. The Pope stood tall and glared. *Tough old bastard.*

"I have every right. And please don't interrupt me in the middle of a diatribe. It's most annoying." Chang straightened his already straight jacket. "Now, why don't we, as the Americans are so fond of saying," he turned to The Pope, "cut the bullshit."

Bishop wondered how they had not only tracked him, but also knew about The Pope, and more importantly suspected that they knew Argento's whereabouts. Kicking down doors seemed excessive. Either this was Chang's usual methodology or they were desperate. Possibly both.

Chang stepped forward and walked slowly in front of them, staring intently as he went. When finished, he swivelled and glared at them all. "You know what I want."

Bishop tilted his head. "What you really really want?"

"What?" Chang's head twisted towards him.

Smiling amenably, Bishop shrugged. "So tell me what you want. What you really really want."

Face creased in confusion, Chang gave a slight shake of his head. "What on Earth are you— You've seen all these guns, yes?" Chang remained unamused. "I could have any one of these men shoot you right now."

Bishop gave a frowning nod. "If that's what you really really want."

Lips pursed, Chang pivoted and walked away. His face grew red. "Jun!"

An assault troop raised his gun, aiming it directly at Bishop's head.

Zhao stared at Bishop wide-eyed. Astonished, she asked quietly, "Do you have a death wish?"

Retaining his affable persona, Bishop whispered, "The man can be rattled. He's serious, under pressure, shows restraint but is prone to outbursts. That means he can be manipulated if handled right."

Zhao stared at Bishop with dual expressions: admiration and the belief that he was completely and utterly mad. Mind racing, Bishop assessed his options. There weren't many. It seemed far too convenient for Chang and his Ministry goons to have arrived in force, ready to obtain the exact same information Bishop was after. Something didn't add up. Did MI6 have a leak? Were they watching The Pope already? But these were questions for another time. First, he had to concentrate on not being shot in the face.

"Tell me, Chang." Bishop's tone was casual, as if no firearms were pointed at him. "You're after something. You say it's in our mutual interest. I'm no expert on these things, but pointing guns at people and threatening to kill them hardly seems conducive to a mutually beneficial partnership."

"Ah, now you sound like a true MI6 operative." Chang grinned. It was an icy, callous expression. "What made you think this was a partnership?" He waved his index finger in Bishop's face. "I said we had the same goal, I did not state we were partners. The mistake was yours."

"You have no right to invade my home like this." It was the first time Ying Yue had spoken. "I am Chinese. This is my house. We were doing nothing but just having dinner. This invasion is illegal." There was no tremble in her voice, despite being the only one of the four with no training, as far as Bishop knew. Regardless, she was tough. Bishop liked her.

"Is that right? Do archaeology professors usually brandish shotguns after dinner? Is this a thing?" Chang issued a bored sigh. "Let us get to the point, shall we? Tell me where Kevin Argento is within one minute or one of you will die."

To emphasise the point, he stared at his watch. The sudden escalation in tension had a different effect on everyone in the room. Bishop's mind reeled, but he squashed the unwieldly thoughts and focused on the situation. He needed to keep everyone safe. He needed to de-escalate the snowballing danger in the room.

He came up blank. He had nothing that would appease Chang. Bishop's thoughts went to the only other avenue available to him. He assessed the position of every combatant in the room. He eyed every armed assault team member, rolling attack scenarios through his head.

The black-clad soldiers remained unmoved, either through training or because they didn't speak English. Ying Yue threw a hand over her mouth as panic invaded her eyes. The Pope grasped her arm, consoling his wife, then he puffed out his chest and clenched his fists. Zhao crouched lower, assuming a fighting stance.

The Pope stepped forward. "You can't possibly expect us to know the whereabouts of—"

"You are my wasting time!" The anger Chang exuded was absolute. But just as suddenly as the rage had appeared, it dissipated. He breathed deeply and straightened his black tie, then tilted his watch so The Pope could see it. "The clock is ticking."

The man was clearly unstable. Calm and humourless one moment, enraged the next, with very little provocation. His wild mood swings made it difficult for Bishop to get a handle on him. He could be bluffing, waiting to see how they reacted. It would be insane to execute one of them without trying to torture or coerce them first. Shooting anyone would be the act of a madman. He had to be bluffing.

Pacing before the four of them, Chang bellowed, "Five."

"Wait, if we could just..." The Pope's tone was imploring.

"Four."

The Pope straightened his back. "This is preposterous."

"Three."

"You're not really going to..."

"Two."

"Wait, please!"

"One." Chang's eyes narrowed on The Pope. "Where is he?"

"I don't know."

"Fine."

Chang clicked his fingers and pointed. A black-clad soldier stepped forward and aimed. Before any of them could utter a word of protest, he fired. In the bare room the sound was deafening.

The body fell. It wasn't like in the movies, where the victim is dramatically propelled backward. They simply collapsed. Lifeless.

No one screamed. No one shouted. For several seconds there was nothing but stunned silence.

Then the world spun up again. The Pope was the first to move. He dashed to the body, cradled her head and wailed. The bullet had entered Ying Yue's body dead centre, obliterating her life instantly. Her face still showed the shock of the moment she died. The only comfort Bishop held was that it was a clean kill. Not that it was any comfort to her inconsolable husband.

The Pope's head snapped to Chang, unhinged fury

carved across his face. The instant transformation was startling. Coiled, The Pope was about to launch himself at the harbinger of his pain when Bishop leapt at him. He tackled the big man to the ground, restrained him face down, arms pinned behind him. The Pope struggled against him, but it was futile. Bishop's grip was as absolute as his determination. The former NSA man soon stopped struggling and resumed his pained wails.

Lips next to The Pope's ear, Bishop whispered quickly. "We'll get the fucking bastard. Soon. Not now. We have to survive if we're going to make him pay. Keep your head. We'll get him. You have my word." Bishop checked that no one had heard his words. "There's a shotgun near your leg."

The Pope looked back at Bishop blankly, his face tear-stained, and nodded. He could comprehend the words spoken. His expression was still hate-filled, but he understood. Whether he was in a state to act was another story. Regardless, they had to fight back.

Chang slapped his hands together like he was about to make a friendly announcement. "Now, where were we?"

"You evil bastard!" Zhao appeared ready to rip Chang's eyes out but restrained herself, thankfully. "She was an innocent. She had nothing to do with this!"

Chang frowned in disagreement and shook his head. "No. No. She wantonly consorted with a plunderer of classified information. Innocence is the luxury of children and the supremely stupid. She was neither. Now… where is Kevin Argento? Tell me in five seconds or someone else dies."

Bishop scanned the assault troops. Their shoulders were more relaxed, their stance not as stiff. Chang walked casually behind them, hands clasped behind his back. All of them held an arrogance in their stance. They'd shown dominance and had broken them.

Or so they thought.

"Five!" Chang's voice boomed.

As quietly as he could, Bishop relinquished his hold on The Pope. He remained in the same position and eyed the troops as his hand slid behind him. None were glancing in his direction, they were all focused either on the wandering Chang or the standing Zhao.

"Four."

Slowly, Bishop's hand slid to the rear of his jeans. Fingers meeting steel, Bishop caught Zhao's eye. She must have seen the look of determination on his face. When she saw where his hand was, she nodded, knowing what was to come.

"Three." Chang was at the back of the room, near where he'd entered.

Bishop drew his pistol. The first to receive a bullet was the young soldier who had put a bullet in Ying Yue. Before he'd even hit the ground, Bishop pivoted and shot his neighbour, who had only started to turn. His head exploded before he even set eyes on Bishop.

The third had far longer to react. His head twisted to Bishop and their eyes locked. His mistake was complacency. Gun slung over his shoulder, he scrambled to seize his weapon. By the time it was in his hands it was too late. Bishop put a bullet in his brain and two in his heart.

The fourth and final foe in the room was an altogether different beast. With ample time to react, he had the drop on Bishop. The assault rifle swung towards him, tucked into the soldier's shoulder: the firing position. Bishop had no time to pivot his pistol. He'd gambled and lost.

The final soldier's head exploded in bone fragments and blood. Beside Bishop, Zhao's pistol hovered, unshaking in her hand. She inhaled deeply, but the breaths weren't panicked, they were focused. They'd taken down all the armed assailants in the room.

Chang leapt through the door he'd entered, towards the other assault troops in the hallway. Without an order being issued, Bishop and Zhao laid down suppression fire and sent them scrambling.

Bishop heaved The Pope up by the collar, dragging him to his feet. "Time to go, big man."

As Bishop pulled the dazed American backwards, Zhao picked up a shotgun, which roared to life, giving them more cover fire. The Pope's face showed nothing but shock, apparently indifferent to the gun battle raging about him.

"Pope, is there another way out of here?" A blank expression was the only reply. "Hey!" Bishop slapped him across the face. It was a callous thing to do to a man who had just lost the love of his life, but those still living needed his help. Mourning was for when you weren't being shot at. "Is there another way out?" The Pope's face was still a blank slate. Bishop was about to slap him again.

"Lawrence." Zhao's voice was soft. "Your wife wouldn't want you to die. You need to survive for her. That's all she'd want. How do we get out of here? You have to live for Ying Yue."

The sound of his wife's name snapped him back to the present. He shook his head, as if to dislodge the malaise, and with a trembling hand pointed towards the rear wall. Taking turns to fire on the entrance doorway behind them, Bishop and Zhao kept the wolves at bay. When one had to reload, the other kept firing. They made a good team.

When they reached the back wall, a disorientated Pope pressed a notch on the frame of a painting of Washington crossing the Delaware. The painting slid silently away to reveal a slim dark passageway, sloping towards the basement.

Zhao expended her last two shotgun shells as she stepped into the passageway. The door slid closed. The earthen walled corridor was dimly lit by gloomy emergency lighting.

"I'm out." Zhao tossed the shotgun to the ground, then extracted her pistol and checked the clip to confirm. "All out."

"I've got…" Bishop checked his clip. "Three left."

"Come." The Pope's voice was raspy. "This way." He moved forward, but stumbled. Holding the wall to steady himself, he moved slowly. "The old missionaries built these secret passages just in case. After the Boxer Rebellion and all. Part of the reason I bought the place. You know, safety." He stopped walking and his face took on a faraway expression. "Kind of silly in retrospect." His expression was humourless and bleak. He continued his walk. "This way, not far. The door won't hold for long."

The Pope pushed open a rickety wooden door at the end of the passage, revealing a dank wine cellar. Hundreds of dusty bottles adorned the brick-lined basement. Bishop moved towards the only door at the far end.

The American gave a *tsk tsk* and shook his head. "Not that way."

He pulled at a wine rack which creaked loudly. As it swung towards them, the entire section of wall pulled away, exposing yet another secret corridor. It appeared far longer than the one they'd escaped through.

"It's an old secret church passage. There's no church any longer, of course, but there's an exit to the golf club." He checked his watch. "It'll be closed now. You'll be fine. Clear out as soon as you can."

Zhao's face was concerned. "You're not coming with us?"

The Pope's face was solemn. "I'm not leaving her."

Bishop grasped the man's wrist. "They'll kill you."

The big American shook his head. "Plenty of hiding places left. Why do you think I chose an old mission building?"

Placing a hand on his shoulder, Bishop eyeballed him. "We can all go together."

The Pope's expression was grim. "I'm a big bastard but believe me, there's plenty of hiding places left. You go. You've done enough here."

Bishop wasn't sure if it was an accusation.

The booming sound of metal against wood told them the soldiers would soon break through the first secret passage.

Zhao went to enter the cramped corridor, but Bishop held back.

He addressed The Pope. "I need the information."

Lips parted, Zhao let out a gasp. "Bishop, he just lost his—"

"Where is he?" Bishop's gaze was hard. "How do I find him?"

Bishop couldn't look at Zhao. He knew she'd be repelled by his callousness, but he was on a mission. He'd come there for information; he wasn't leaving without it.

The Pope was dazed, his eyes unfocused. "What, what?"

Bishop placed his hands on the big man's shoulders. "Argento. How do I find him?"

The distant pounding grew louder. Shouts could be heard.

The Pope, still dazed, focused on Bishop. "Changzhou. He's in Changzhou."

"That's all, a city?"

Staring at him blankly, The Pope blinked several times. Patting himself down, he added, "No, I have a…" He pulled out a crumpled Post-It note. "…a phone number. He called me from it. It may have been a burner, I don't know." He stuffed it into Bishop's palm.

"Thank you."

As Bishop went to move into the passage, it was Zhao's turn to stay. She studied the tragic figure of The Pope.

"Are you going to be alright?"

Blank-faced, The Pope turned to her. "I'll be okay… I just need…"

"Time?" she asked.

"No." He shook his head. "For you to survive to kill every last one of those sons of bitches."

A crashing sound told them the troops had smashed through the barrier. They had mere seconds.

"We'll do our best." Bishop grabbed Zhao's arm and pulled her in. Turning back to The Pope, he said, "You need to go."

The Pope nodded. "Find him. Remember your promise." He closed the wine rack door behind them. It clicked shut, leaving them in the completely dark underground passage.

Bishop heard faint footsteps and the distant creak of a door. Several seconds later, the deafening sound of trampling footsteps could be heard bursting into the wine cellar. Shouts in Mandarin filled the confined space, overlapping, adding to the confusion. They soon trampled away, leaving only stillness behind.

In a low whisper, Zhao asked, "Now what?"

Turning on the torch on his phone, Bishop strode down the passageway as quietly as he could. "Now we finish what we came here to do."

CHAPTER SIX

The exit into the golf club was uneventful. The tunnel ended in a rickety shed on the edge of a forested area near the driving range. As The Pope had promised, the club was closed, and they made their way to the main road without challenge.

They stuck to the shadows, avoiding the light of the three-quarter moon. Bishop noted Zhao's sullen demeanour; she stomped along, hands thrust deep in her pockets. Reassessing his evaluation, he determined that Zhao wasn't sullen, more like a petulant teen. Steam was virtually coming out of her ears.

Matching her pace as they rounded a corner, he tried to appear casual. "Have I done something wrong?"

She skidded to a halt. "Something wrong!" she shrieked, then lowered her voice. "Something wrong? You left him behind. He's most likely dead by now. You didn't even try and convince him to come with us."

"I offered, he said no." Bishop's manner was neutral. He didn't have time for this.

"You could have dragged him away."

"Did you see the size of the man? Not likely."

Bishop checked his phone. There was an all-night karaoke bar three miles away. While they'd still been underground he'd contacted the MI6 Beijing station, and they were dispatching a trustworthy local driver who would collect their bags, smuggle them out of the city and get them to Changzhou. While they waited, Bishop planned to pay cash for a private booth and lay low.

He glanced at his partner, still fuming. "What?"

"Why didn't you act sooner?" Zhao's arms flailed. "Ying Yue would still be alive if you'd acted sooner."

That one stung. She might be a crack shot, but Zhao still had a lot to learn about field work. "I didn't know if Chang was going to go through with it. He hadn't even negotiated, he should have been bluffing. It was madness."

"And now an innocent woman is dead!"

"You're being irrational."

"Don't you dare call me an irrational woman." Zhao stabbed a finger at him. "Don't you dare."

Coming to a halt before a closed drycleaner, Bishop sighed and raised his hands defensively. In a calm voice, he replied, "I'm not particularly fond of that tired, condescending cliché. That wasn't my intent. I merely stated that you were being hysterical. Which, I might add, was a fact based on your tone and volume, rather than a sexist platitude."

"Would it be sexist if I punched you in the dick right now?" Her face carried anger, but around the periphery there were tiny fractures, amusement at her own words.

"Look, I'm going to be honest with you, I'd prefer if you didn't." He threw her his best boyish grin. "The bruising would be unseemly."

Zhao raised an eyebrow. "I can imagine."

"Can you now?"

"Oh yes." Zhao tilted her head. "And I have a big imagination."

It may have been the adrenaline talking, but Zhao appeared hungry. The sudden change in her demeanour was startling. From aggravation to temptress in a matter of seconds. She almost purred. Conscious that their pursuers were still close, Bishop motioned that they should continue on their way. Keeping pace, Zhao walked closer. The occasional touches of their hands as they walked may have been accidental, but there was no apology.

And just like that, it seemed their animosity had evaporated into the cold night air. If there was indeed a new sense of sexual tension, Bishop did his best to pay it no heed. There were more pressing matters at hand.

The first was getting to Changzhou. The next was finding Kevin Argento and finishing this mission any way he could.

The karaoke bar was even more appalling than Bishop had imagined. He and Zhao had huddled in a small booth for two hours, waiting for their driver. The dark sleazy room came complete with soft leather couches and a knowing wink from the proprietor. The ample supply of alcohol helped marginally with the long wait. As did Zhao's willing company. Although, no matter how many times she'd begged, Bishop had refused her persistent requests.

There was no way he was going to sing karaoke. A man must maintain his dignity.

Zhao's method of dealing with Ying Yue's death was evidently to order three extremely large pizzas and proceed to get very drunk and pretend it hadn't happened. Bishop, on the other hand, went over the events in minute detail, over and over again. Between sips of a cheap Johnnie Walker knock-off, he filed his report and relived every action in excruciating detail. How he could have addressed the situation differently, acted quicker. How he could have saved her. Most of all, Bishop recalled all he could about the cruelty of the man named Chang.

Bishop tried calling The Pope several times, but he didn't answer. He wondered if the NSA man had survived. The old bastard was clever and resourceful, but also in deep personal pain. Though it would be a stretch to label their relationship friendly, Bishop hoped the big man had made it out.

At one am, their driver arrived. Li was young but with old features, like an old soul. With a friendly smile, he escorted the two to his Lexus purposefully. In no time, they were heading away under the cover of night. Li chatted amiably about nothing in particular, an attempt to put them at ease, Bishop could tell. One could easily confuse his friendly demeanour for naivety, but from the way he sized them both up, subtly observed the movement of their clothing for concealed weapons, Bishop could see there was more to Li than it first appeared.

Already tired from the night's escapades and ample quantities of booze, Zhao removed her jacket and rolled it into a ball. She leaned her head against the car door and burrowed into a comfortable position. Bishop imagined she'd be out in no time. The soft lighting of the streetlights gave her features an otherworldly glow. She was an attractive woman. Bishop shook off his wayward thoughts. For one, now was not the time.

For another—and this was most unexpected—the moment he visualised a more intimate partnership with Zhao, a different image leapt into his mind. The figure of an extremely pissed off Tessa glaring at him as he boarded the plane to Beijing. Despite her scowl, she was still amazingly beautiful. Why had she interrupted his thoughts so? They'd broken up two years ago, she should no longer have a hold on him. And yet, there she was, dancing before his tired eyes.

"Where to, boss?" Li's tone remained friendly.

"Don't call me boss." Bishop was tired, but he didn't want his briskness to be confused with rudeness. "I say that merely because we're colleagues. We're on the same mission."

Li beamed. "Apologies, it comes with the driver act." He nodded to Bishop in the rear-view mirror.

"Where are you from, Li?"

"Beijing embassy."

Bishop smiled. "Where from originally."

Through the rear-view mirror, Li grinned. "Liverpool. Mum and Dad fled after Tiananmen Square. In the first week after joining '6 an instructor said, hey, you look Chinese, do you speak Chinese? Like Chinese is a language. Fucken' dick." Realising what he'd just said, he quickly added, "Shit. Sorry."

With that kind of uncontrolled conversation, Bishop could tell the kid wasn't field experienced. Far from it. The way he'd first sized them up showed he had at least some training, but it appeared he'd rarely used it.

"What's your function, normally, when you're not driving folks around in the middle of the night?" Bishop kept his tone light.

There was a pause while Li turned red. "I fix the servers when they go down."

Bishop peered out the window to the dark, sparsely populated streets. "Not many servers out here."

"Yeah, kinda got stuck with it, to be honest. Half the

embassy are down with the flu. I drew the short straw. No offence."

"None taken."

Bishop wasn't planning on getting into any firefights on the drive, so he didn't need a lethal killing machine at the wheel. Li would do fine.

"What's our destination?" Li seemed eager to change the subject.

"Changzhou."

"Yeah, I already got that, but where? Changzhou's a big place."

"That's all I have for now."

MI6 were attempting to trace the number The Pope had given Bishop, but apparently it was next to impossible on a foreign telephone system. There was a chance they might be able to use satellites if he was on the phone for long enough, but even the IT boffins thought it unlikely. It was a long shot at best.

"Well, you have," Li checked the display on the dash, "eleven hours to get a bit more specific. I suggest you two get comfortable back there. It's a long drive."

Li tapped the volume control and the car was filled with some kind of dance music with deep rhythms and layered melodies.

Bishop rubbed his tired eyes. "What's this?"

Li grinned. "John 00 Fleming."

"Wait… you work at MI6 and listen to an artist called John 00 Fleming?"

Li's brow crumpled and he seemed hurt. "You don't like trance?" Sitting up, he brightened. "Want something else? I have everything, just name it. Techno, melodic, goa, prog, trip, psy, whatever. Just no breaks or dub, okay?"

Bishop stared. "I'm pretty sure you made half of those up."

For the first time Bishop realised how exhausted he felt. Eyelids feeling like lead, he leaned back against the headrest and the deep thrum of Li's music dragged him towards sleep. The last image he saw in his mind was the glee on Chang's face when Ying Yue fell to the floor.

"Wait, wait… You know it?" Zhao's face creased with scepticism. "You're making it up."

Bishop raised an eyebrow. "Born from an egg on a mountaintop. The punkiest monkey that ever popped!" He followed it up by extending his index and middle fingers and brushing them briskly as he blew out.

"Holy shit!" Zhao covered her mouth. Bishop wasn't sure if it was shock or the fact that she'd sworn in front of a superior officer.

"I have no flippin' clue what you guys are on about." Li changed lanes in the increasingly busy morning traffic. "Are you guys speaking in code?"

"Monkey," Zhao said, mouth agape at Bishop. "A really old Japanese TV show from the 80s. I had no idea it got to the West. That's awesome."

"It was badly dubbed and ridiculous. I used to watch it in my pyjamas when I was a kid."

Zhao poked Bishop in the arm. "I'm going to have to rethink my whole assessment of you, Mr Charles Bishop."

"What was the initial assessment?"

"Oh man, you seriously don't want to know."

Her smile was dazzling. Bishop was really warming to Zhao. She was a dependable agent, funny and engaging. And she did have the most amazing eyes. For a brief moment, he let himself think about spending more time with her, in a more intimate setting. He let his mind float around in the daydream for a while.

"Anyone else hungry?"

Zhao's question was a welcome one, and not unexpected. It also slapped Bishop's wandering mind back into place. Until she'd asked the question, Bishop hadn't even thought of food. Now he realised he was starving.

They pulled into a roadside petrol station, similar in appearance to ones the world over. The main differences were the choices of takeaway breakfast. Zhao took the lead and returned to the car with a selection of steamed buns, boiled eggs and congee. As they ate, Bishop noticed something in the distance.

"Is that Changzhou? I thought it was further away." The more Bishop analysed it, the odder the city appeared. There was something peculiar about it, but he couldn't put his finger on what.

Li glanced up and shook his head. "Nah, man. That's a ghost city."

"Right." Bishop paused, then frowned. "A what?"

"Ghost city. You know, a city they built that no one lives in. A shit-ton of them have popped up all over China for a whole mess of reasons. There were these incentives by local governments to finance real estate construction and stuff. You know, gotta build, gotta build! Also, China's a little hooked on this real estate construction binge. Fuck actual demand, right?"

Bishop finally realised what had seemed wrong about it. "There are no roads to it."

"Why would there be? No one lives there, why build a road to it?"

With his hand above his eyes, Bishop stared into the far distance. "The place is huge. It'd have to house at least fifty thousand. So, there's all those high rises, internal roads, and it's all abandoned?"

Li slapped him on the back. "Welcome to China, buddy. It doesn't have to make sense, it just has to be huge."

After he'd eaten, Bishop tried The Pope once more. No answer. He then checked on communications from Vauxhall Cross.

"London's come up with nothing," Bishop said, referring to the trace on Argento's phone.

"Nothing… how is that possible?" Li said incredulously, half a steamed bun in his mouth. "Who told you that?"

Bishop scrolled down on the email and found the name at the bottom of the page. "Pillar."

"Fucken' Pillar." Li shook his head and swallowed. "The only reason that douchebag has a job is because his aunt is in the JIC. That fucken guy."

"Do you have a better way?"

"Of course." Li reached back and pulled a laptop from the seat pocket behind him. "Look, there's some really old legacy tech out there in the global phone network. There's this thing called SS7, Signalling System 7, yeah?" He flipped open the laptop and swiped his finger to log in. "Built way back in the seventies. It allows users to move from one network to another. Worked well back in the day, but now it has more fucken' holes than the plot of a *Transformers* movie. See, to hack into the Chinese network, all you have to do is impersonate another carrier making a legit request for info about a customer. Pillar's probably using access request protocols that have already been plugged up; it got too hard and he gave up. Dickhead's probably getting paid ten times what I am. I bet you a month's wage he couldn't find porn on the internet." Li tracked his finger about the laptop's pad and typed in various commands.

Not following any of what Li was saying, Bishop asked, "What are you doing now?"

"I'm piggybacking the Israeli ULIN system. Great little hackers, the Israelis, really know their shit. Ha! See?" Li pointed to the screen, which to Bishop appeared the same as it had a minute ago. "We're in! Right, now give me the number."

Bishop handed Li the slip of paper and he plugged in the number, then stretched. "This will take a minute or two."

Bishop was pleased with his initial assessment of Li; there was indeed more going on under the surface. "It appears your talents are wasted as a driver."

"Yathink?" With an expression of shock, Li composed himself. "Shit. Sorry. Meant to say, thank you for saying so. I'm out of practice talking to, you know, actual people."

Zhao observed the exchange with amusement. She bit into a steamed bun and watched the show before her unfold.

The laptop pinged and Li hunched as he clicked away. "There!" He pointed at the map before him. "He's still in Changzhou. Geographical area accurate to within..." He squinted. "Five hundred metres. I can probably refine it a little for you, but that's your guy. We can be up in his face in an hour and a half."

"Can they trace you?" Bishop checked his watch. "The Chinese, I mean. Hacking into their system?"

"I'm like a ghost's ghost." On seeing the blank expression on their faces, Li added, "That made more sense in my head." The faint sound of passing cars filled the silence. He went on. "For all they know it was a legitimate request, of which they get tens of thousands per hour. Completely untraceable, even if they knew what they were looking for. Like I said, old legacy systems, not designed for the twenty-first century."

"I have one question." Zhao wiped her hands on a napkin. "Why are we still talking? We've got an ex-MI6 agent to find."

Li and Bishop exchanged glances.

"She has a point." Li closed the laptop. "Let's get moving."

They packed away the remnants of their food and put on their seatbelts. As Li pulled out of the car park, Bishop said, "It's like we're on a quest." He cast Zhao a sideways glance. "And I'm Monkey and you're Tripitaka. Li can be Sandy."

"No way!" Zhao pretended to be offended. "I'm totally Monkey. You can be Sandy."

Bishop frowned and shook his head. "I've changed my mind. I'm Monkey and you're Pigsy."

"Pigsy!" Zhao gave him a playful whack on the arm. "Screw you!" She laughed adorably.

Li pulled into traffic. "I still have no idea what you lot are on about."

The park was quiet. The low afternoon clouds seem to have scared off most people. The park seemed new; the many trees making up the mini forest at the centre were not fully grown and the lush green grass was weed-free, as if only recently laid. The carefully manicured edges of the park led to a surrounding wall of identical double-storey homes, the only distinguishing feature between them being the plants in each garden and the luxury car in each driveway. A smattering of people scurried about, but mostly it was green grass, trees and the occasional dog.

"You're sure?" Bishop scowled. This wasn't what he expected.

In the driver's seat, huddled over his laptop, Li nodded but didn't reply immediately, too busy clicking and typing. Eventually he raised his head and squinted towards the park. "He's in there. For sure."

"Maybe he left his phone behind?" Zhao shared Bishop's scepticism.

"Nah." Li shook his head. "The signal's shifting. He's moving, that's for sure. Argento's in the park. One hundred per cent."

"Why can't we see him, then?"

Li turned, his face uncertain. "Invisibility cloak?"

Bishop grunted. "Well, let's get a closer look then."

The three exited the car and braced against the chill. Bishop tucked his two pistols in the back of his jeans. He may have been doubtful, but he wasn't taking any chances. They crossed the road and scanned the area. The clouds were getting darker; a cold front was moving in.

Laptop open, Li trudged through the park, indicating where to go like a high-tech water diviner. Bishop folded his arms. Kevin Argento wasn't a man easily missed. Six two, stocky build, the man would stand out in Trafalgar Square, let alone an uninhabited park in the middle of China. The more Li increased his pace, the more cynical Bishop became.

"There, fifty metres, directly ahead!"

Li's excitement was not shared by Zhao. "Where?" She scanned the deserted stretch of park in front of them. "Behind the dog?"

Li glanced up. "Oh." His face dropped. "Uh, see, that's the thing. Um, I think the signal... I... okay, it's the dog. The signal's coming from the dog."

They all looked at one another. The three of them had come all this way, spent hours in the car, only to have their hopes dashed. The scruffy brown mutt sat on the grass and tilted his head curiously at the newcomers. Around its neck was a shiny new black collar, and gaffer taped to it was a rectangular shape, roughly the size of a small mobile phone. The dog growled as they approached.

"Is it possible he turned into a dog?" Li's attempt at levity fell as flat as a two-dimensional pancake. "I'm just asking, sheesh."

Bishop sighed heavily. "Just for that, you're in charge of catching the dog."

"The dog? Why?"

"Argento is obviously playing with us, attaching the phone to this mutt." Bishop watched the dog more closely. He was certain it snarled at him in particular. "Argento's deliberately sent us off on a wild goose chase. I want to know why. In order to find out," he turned to Li, "you're going to have to catch the dog."

Li frowned. "He's a stray."

"Appears that way."

"He looks angry."

"Have you seen *my* face?" Bishop raised an eyebrow.

"I'm pretty sure he has rabies. Is he foaming at the mouth? I think he's foaming at the mouth."

"Li. Get the damn dog."

For the next five minutes Li chased the poor unsuspecting dog around the park. He tried everything—creeping up slowly, rushing it, lying on the ground—but only succeeded in garnering bemused expressions from passers-by.

Eventually Li staggered back. With his hands on his knees, he panted. "There's no catching the little bastard. He's an escape artist. Yeah, I'm calling him Houdini dog."

Without a word, Zhao went to the car and returned

with a small package. The apparent Houdini dog jogged towards her and sniffed the leftover steamed bun. He took a tentative lick, and when no one told him off, a tiny bite. Zhao placed the bun on the ground. As he chomped away, Zhao put on rubber gloves and unhooked the dog's collar. She cast Li an incredulous look.

"I'm surprised," Bishop said, arms crossed.

"That I could figure out how to get the phone?"

Bishop shook his head. "No. That you had leftover food."

"Funny man."

Bishop suspected there was no need for the gloves. Even under the layers of tape, he could smell the ammonia his old mentor had used. There would be no prints.

Zhao gave the dog a pat, then they returned to the warmer confines of the car. She cut away the tape to uncover a Huawei mobile phone. It required a PIN to gain access, close to impossible to hack into.

They stared at the phone. They'd come so far for nothing. It was a dead end.

Bishop stared out into the park as the gloomy clouds rolled in, his thoughts equally dark. His mission parameters were straightforward: take down Kevin Argento. His feelings on the matter, however, were nowhere near as simple. As much as he tried to deny it, there was a tiny sense of relief that his old mentor hadn't been in the park. Although he was almost sure he could pull the trigger when the time came, there was still an element of doubt. That concerned him more than anything.

None of them said a word, each lost in their own headspace. Suddenly the phone in Zhao's hand buzzed, making them jump. A text message. Words appeared on the lock screen.

Frowning, Zhao held the phone up to Bishop. "What do you make of this?"

She held up the phone. The message, from a blocked number, read: *You should have stayed down, son.*

Scanning the rows of identical houses, Bishop knew he wouldn't spot his old mentor, but he'd been seen. Argento knew his old pupil was after him. That made things far more problematic. And dangerous. Kevin Argento had taught Bishop everything he knew, which unfortunately meant he was acquainted with Bishop's tricks, too.

The hunter had become the prey.

They drove away from the park on high alert. Bishop directed Li to double back, increase and decrease speed, take three right turns and then turn down a one-way street. He also had him stop at a green light, then take off as the light turned red. None of these manoeuvres revealed a tail. They proceeded towards their hotel.

In the back of the Lexus, Bishop stared out the window. The wide streets of Changzhou were relatively free of traffic; the gloomy Sunday afternoon weather seemed to have scared off most drivers. A smattering of rain fell against the passenger window.

The text message was laced with intent. A threat. Or a promise. Argento had sent a message telling Bishop he knew he was after him. Argento didn't have to send it, but he did. Did that mean he wanted Bishop to back off because of their past friendship, or was he letting him know it was okay for Bishop to be pursuing him? Or did he intend something else entirely?

As he gazed vacantly out the window, Bishop caught the glance of another driver in a black Buick Envision.

For a moment, their eyes met. The other driver's stare lasted just a fraction of a moment longer than Bishop was comfortable with. Every instinct he had told him something was wrong.

Head darting around, Bishop found three more identical black SUVs keeping pace.

"Let me drive."

In the front seat, Li chuckled. "Sure, man. I'll just let go of the wheel, shall I?"

Eyes on the surrounding vehicles, Bishop's hand instinctively went to the gun in his shoulder holster. "At the next set of lights, get into the passenger seat as fast as you can. I'll leap over."

"What? You're serious? Why?"

"See the four matching black Buicks? We've got tails. I give it two minutes before they make their move."

"But… but, you said all that counter-surveillance stuff we did showed that we weren't being followed." Li's head darted around.

"Keep your eyes forward," Bishop snapped. "We weren't followed." Bishop caught Zhao's eye. Like him, she checked her weapon, game face on. "They found us afterwards."

"But how?" Li's face was wrapped with apprehension.

It was a good question. It took Bishop all of five seconds to figure it out. "Son of a motherless goat."

"What?"

"Give me the dog phone."

Bishop held out his hand. Confused, Zhao slapped it into his palm. Bishop opened the window and, without looking, flung the phone out of the car.

"We traced the phone to its source. I'm betting Chang and his goons did exactly the same thing. Now, pull up at the lights, we'll swap places there."

What Bishop didn't mention was that in order for Chang to have obtained the number, one of two things would have to have happened. Either The Pope had given them up or Chang's goons had somehow managed to extract information from his fried servers. Either way, they were made.

One of the SUVs had manoeuvred around traffic and was in front of them, already slowing for a red light. Li slowed at the intersection with a panicked expression. Bishop leapt into the front seat, gently pushed Li aside and slapped his seatbelt in place. The other two quickly followed his example. Bishop eyed the black Buick in front and the two flanking them. They were boxed in. In the rear-view mirror Bishop watched the lead Buick at the rear hurtle towards them, showing no sign of slowing. They were about to be rammed at full speed.

"Everyone, hold onto something. This is going to hurt."

CHAPTER SEVEN

Seconds before impact, Bishop hit the buttons to lower all the windows and threw the car into reverse. They were pinned in by the three other huge Buicks, but he spun the wheel so the rear panel of their Lexus scraped the SUV to their left. The grating sound of metal and plastic being wrenched apart barely registered for Bishop. He floored it. The driver on the left hadn't had time to counter his move, so when the lead vehicle hit, it was a glancing blow rather than a fatal one.

Outside was mayhem. The lead SUV ricocheted off Bishop's car into the vehicle on the right, which had taken the brunt of the crash, before careening into the intersection. All three cars had been propelled forward into other vehicles. Shouts and screams and car horns intermingled in a cacophony of chaos.

In Bishop's car, the airbags had deployed, filling the cabin with fine white powder. The open windows meant the powder would soon dissipate, and they weren't covered in glass fragments either. The car was still running. Bishop pushed down the deflating airbag and threw the car into gear.

Over his shoulder, Bishop glanced at the vehicle on the right, the one that had sustained the most damage. A stunned Chang glared back at him with a shocked expression, no doubt wondering how his men had botched a simple boxing-in manoeuvre. Bishop had no time to gloat.

Tyres screeching, he reversed into a gap in the traffic which had formed in the crash's aftermath. Slowing only to let a concerned citizen race towards the crash scene, Bishop stamped on the accelerator. Speeding up, he wove through the slowing traffic, drivers wary of the accident before them.

Blocked in by the carnage, Chang's vehicle wasn't going anywhere. All around, drivers exited their vehicles, either to assess the damage or looking to assist. Another of Chang's hench-cars wasn't as restricted. Apparently not caring that the red-coated Samaritan was behind the car, the vehicle slammed into him. The force of the impact sent the poor man sprawling, knocked to the ground in the path of the SUV. The last Bishop saw in his rear-view mirror was the man's red coat disappearing beneath the Buick as it sped after them.

Bishop focused on the rain-drenched road before him. The wheels were out of alignment after the crash and the steering wheel shuddered in his hands. They had evaded the trap, but gained only seconds. They needed far more than that. Beside him, Li appeared to be hurtling towards a nervous breakdown. Zhao was shaken, but doing her best to keep her cool.

Behind them, Bishop saw a single black SUV weaving through the traffic in pursuit. It seemed they'd narrowed the odds, but not by enough. There could be more pursuers, and they were running out of time. Outmanned and outgunned in a vast country with very few safe havens, they had no support and no escape route. They had to get off the roads.

"Zhao, fold down the back seat and grab my case. We'll need guns—oh, and grenades, we'll need those too."

Nodding tentatively, Zhao did as she was asked. As she folded down the back seat, she asked, "What's the plan?"

Bishop scanned the road signs and searched for pursuing vehicles. He grinned. "Who wants to go see some dinosaurs?"

"Did you say...?" Li stared at him, concern etched into every pore. "You sure you don't want me to drive?"

The Lexus didn't slow as it approached the immense car park. The lateness of the day and the atrocious weather meant it was mostly vacant. Bishop hurtled towards the entrance at a reckless speed. Skidding to a halt at the closest park, his seatbelt was off before the engine died.

The Changzhou Dinosaur Park was like a tacky Disneyland knockoff. Over the tall fake rock walls of the entrance, the heads of several dinosaurs could be seen intermingling with rollercoasters and assorted rides bobbing up and down.

They'd last seen the remaining black SUV two kilometres back. Bishop had managed to build up a small gap, but he knew it would never last. They couldn't outrun them. They'd have to outsmart them.

They leapt out of the car; everyone had their instructions. Zhao handed out weapons. Bishop had his two pistols, but grabbed extra ammunition. Zhao had a snub-nosed submachine gun under her large coat. Li was given a pistol the same as Bishop's. As an MI6 employee, he would have received some rudimentary weapons training. Before she closed the case, Bishop pointed to a large hunting knife. Zhao handed it to him, then slammed the door shut.

As Li scanned the car park for incoming hostiles, Zhao passed Bishop three hand grenades. He pocketed one, then leaned through the open window and carefully placed the other two between the base of the seat and the door on the driver's side. Cautiously, he removed the pins.

Straightening up, he caught sight of a black Buick SUV careening into the car park. "Let's go, kids. Now remember, stick together, don't talk to strangers and no rides just after you've eaten."

Li turned to Bishop as they jogged towards the vacant entrance. "Sometimes I wonder if you're brilliant or totally mental."

"You and me both, kid."

The grand entrance to the park was gaudy in the extreme, a heady mix of nineteenth-century pavilion, *Jurassic Park* rip-off and something from *The Flintstones*. Even at the entrance, there were signs for KFC and McDonald's. The theme to this park wasn't dinosaurs; it was tackiness.

Bishop stuffed a wad of cash in Zhao's hand as they approached the ticket booth. When Zhao tried to hand over the money, the woman in the ticket booth had a quick discussion with her. Most probably the attendant with the pterodactyl on her hat was telling Zhao the park was about to close. Smiling the whole time, Zhao seemed to convince the attendant it was fine. Li and Bishop kept an eye on the rapidly approaching SUV.

Tickets in hand, Zhao nodded towards the fake rock turnstiles. Bishop could hear muffled dinosaur roars, squeals of delight and that tinny sideshow music that was the same the world over.

The young woman at the turnstile scanned their tickets with soulless eyes and said something that Bishop assumed was "Have a nice day" with as much enthusiasm as someone placing a death-row lunch order.

They slipped through the barrier as five black-coated men wove through the parked cars. The men seemed to have only one goal: the Lexus. No weapons were drawn, but their stern, focused faces were enough to scare anyone within a twenty-metre radius. Bishop knew they would be armed with far more than a scowl.

From behind the steel railing, Bishop was able to observe the goings on in the car park without being seen. Outside, a man with an expensive haircut slowed his pace, his hand deep inside his coat pocket. Further back, a smaller team was led by a severe-looking guy with a shaved head. Mr Shaved Head held back, perhaps wondering why the vehicle had been left unlocked with the windows down.

Mr Expensive Haircut didn't share his comrade's caution. He approached with military precision, keeping an eye out for external threats.

Li poked his head around curiously, but Bishop pushed it back. Three of the team crept closer to the car as Mr Expensive Haircut bent down to use the door handle. Bishop held his breath.

The first explosion was quickly followed by another. Flames burst skyward, followed by excruciating screams. The panicked shouts and cries of pain intermingled with a third explosion that Bishop took to be the fuel tank. All evidence of who they were had been incinerated, along with several of their assailants.

Motioning to his team, Bishop pointed towards the heart of the park. They wove their way through fake alleys of garish souvenir stores and Mr Bean coffee shops. Glancing back at the entrance, Bishop saw bewildered staff surveying the billowing black fireball that snaked into the darkened sky. Their dumbfounded demeanours would soon change. Bishop was counting on it. He turned and trotted away from the mounting chaos.

The park was as kitschy as the entrance, and consisted of endless statues of historically apocryphal dinosaurs. Some had feathered headdresses, others wore harnesses on their backs like elephant transport. Other dinosaurs were ridden by spear-carrying lizard men.

As they jogged, Bishop mused. "I'm beginning to doubt the historical accuracy of this park."

"Why ever would you say that?" Zhao pointed to a giant statue of King Kong lifting a tramcar full of squealing tourists. "Seems completely accurate to me."

A loud, thunderous rumble reverberated throughout the park. Seconds later, a deluge of rain sent tourists scurrying for cover. The MI6 team kept their pace; Bishop took the lead.

As rain bucketed down, reducing visibility, Bishop searched the edges of the cobblestone pathways until he found what he was after. In a far corner, a stand selling balloons and inflatable dinosaurs stood abandoned, its owner having wisely rushed out of the pelting rain. Without breaking stride, Bishop extracted the remaining grenade, pulled the pin and tossed it under the stand. All three sprinted away, getting as far from the stand as they could. They managed to reach a clump of drenched tourists huddled under a giant stegosaurus before detonation.

The explosion echoed around the park, igniting the tanks of helium and creating a massive orange flash. Li and Zhao flung themselves to the ground, as did every nearby tourist, except Bishop. He remained standing, scanning the rain-drenched park for anyone wearing a black coat who seemed undaunted by the explosion.

He found one.

Only one, standing alone in a long black coat. Like many others in the park, he glared at the billowing smoke from the explosion. But unlike the tourists, he seemed to know it wasn't a random gas tank explosion. The man with the shaved head examined the crowd, his gaze lingering on any Western faces. He hadn't spotted Bishop yet, but he would soon enough.

Most of the tourists under the dinosaur were dazed, unsure what to do. Leaning down, Bishop spoke to Li and Zhao. "We need to move." To Li, Bishop said, "I want you to direct people to the food court over there."

Li nodded and yelled, "Zhè tiáo lù!"

Eagerly following the one person who seemed to have a clue, the clump of twenty tourists beneath the fibreglass dinosaur followed Li as he trotted away. Using the mass of scrambling people as cover, Bishop kept his eye on the black-coated adversary who faced the other way. As the crowd stumbled towards him, he glanced at them, then turned his attention elsewhere. Bishop struggled to avoid being seen. Tall and blond, he had to crouch low in the jostling crowd, receiving elbows to the head for his trouble.

With difficulty, Bishop kept an eye on the guy in the black coat. He was the same man Bishop had seen holding back in the car park. Wisely, as it turned out. As Bishop approached, he could make out the coiled wire behind Mr Shaved Head's right ear. Bishop imagined that by now the park would have a smattering of black-coated assailants, assuming the others had managed to get their vehicles free. They may even be at full strength. Well, apart from the ones who'd been blown up.

Mr Shaved Head gave the encroaching crowd another

cursory glance, but took more interest in the rest of the park, presumably thinking Bishop and his team wouldn't be part of the crowd. In Mr Shaved Head's defence, that would normally be true. The man's hand was on his earpiece, his head tilted towards his left shoulder. Bishop sighed. Amateur. You never outwardly convey the presence of your comms equipment.

Not wanting to panic the crowd further or attract more attention, Bishop's fingers closed around the hilt of the hunting knife. Firing a weapon in an already startled populous would bring more black coats running. He would use stealth. Go old school.

Approaching from behind, Bishop bounded towards the man, unsheathing the knife as he ran. His first stroke sliced the wire from the man's earpiece. Before he could react, Mr Shaved Head had a knife to his throat.

"Hands where I can see them. Take it very easy, buddy."

Raising his hands, the man gave a slight nod. Most likely the guy didn't speak English. It didn't matter. Bishop's tone was clear: do as I say, or you die. He got the gist.

With the knife tucked into Mr Shaved Head's coat, pressed against his heart, the two strode awkwardly towards a narrow alleyway. Zhao caught up. She seemed alarmed, but said nothing.

The rain had doubled down, drenching anyone still out in the open. The alley was awash with rain, which cascaded down the red bricks of the buildings. Finally, clear of prying eyes, Bishop tugged the pistol from Mr Shaved Head's jacket and pushed him forward. He hit the wall and spun. The collision with the wall split his lip, but the blood was immediately washed away by the rain. The man didn't seem to care. His furious eyes told Bishop there was only one thing on his mind.

"Do you work for Chang?" Bishop had to yell to be heard over the pelting rain.

The man's facial features didn't alter.

Bishop nodded at Zhao to translate. She did exactly that, albeit reluctantly. She seemed unimpressed with Bishop's tactics. Still the man didn't acknowledge the question. Bishop realised he may need more encouragement.

"Ask him again." Bishop held the knife aloft, rain splashing against the blade. "Tell him this time I said please."

Zhao shouted the words, her gaze anxiously darting between the two men. Eyeing the knife, Mr Shaved Head frowned and then nodded. With narrowed eyes, his hand slowly slipped deep into his coat. In spite of Bishop's warnings, he extricated a knife of his own. A malevolent sneer creased his lips as he tilted his head and shrugged, issuing a silent challenge.

Bishop returned the sneer. He tossed the knife up and caught it, blade down. It was better for close-quarters fighting.

Zhao growled. "We don't have time for this."

"Sure we do." Bishop circled the other man, a slow deadly dance. "Plus, this guy thinks he's tough. He needs to be taken down a few pegs before he'll be a Chatty Cathy."

Bishop's knife fighting skills were a bit rusty, but he knew you never made the first move. You sized up your opponent, saw how they moved, their footwork, how they worked their blade.

Mr Shaved Head didn't know any of that. Far too eager, he lunged at Bishop, telegraphing his first move and overextending himself. With an upward sweep of his knife, Bishop sliced into his opponent's arm. The blade made short work of the coat. A flash of red told Bishop he'd found his mark.

With a cry of pain, the man recoiled, cradling his arm. Raindrops splattering against his bald head as he assessed the damage. With a scream he lunged wildly at Bishop, who sidestepped the attack. Ducking low, Bishop slashed at the man's exposed torso.

Staggering forward, the black-coated assailant clutched his side and screamed in agony. He flipped open his coat, his white shirt split open, soaked in red. Even the deluge of rain wasn't enough to wash away the torrent of blood oozing from the six-inch gash in his side.

Glancing up, Mr Shaved Head gritted his teeth.

Bishop shook his head. "Don't."

He didn't listen. The assailant inelegantly sprang towards Bishop, knife held high. His move was slow and awkward. Pivoting where he stood, Bishop once again side-stepped the clumsy attack. Eye on the knife, he grasped the man's wrist and thrust his own knife deep into his forearm, the blade slicing its way between the ulna and radius.

The attacker dropped to his knees, screaming in pain. His knife fell to the soaked ground. Bishop towered above him, hand still on the knife handle.

"Why is Chang after us?"

Through his immense pain, the man shook his head.

Bishop pushed the knife further into his arm. The blade came through the other side, eliciting a pitiful scream. Bishop nodded to Zhao to translate. She did so, concern in her eyes and an expression of distaste on her face.

Mr Shaved Head was close to passing out. He spat blood and stared at Bishop with hatred in his eyes. "Because you'll lead us to Argento."

So, he did speak English after all.

"Then why ram our car?"

It didn't make sense to Bishop. He assumed whoever had traced the phone would patiently wait for them to find Kevin Argento. Why show their hand by attacking the car?

Mr Shaved Head's eyes darted between Bishop and Zhao. "My employer grows impatient. He can no longer wait for you to blindly stumble upon your prey. You will be bait."

Bishop nodded. "What if we don't want to be bait?"

Mr Shaved Head smiled, revealing bloodied teeth. "The worm rarely has a choice."

"Ah yes, but the early worm gathers no moss."

Confusion creased the pale man's face. "What?"

"The worm may turn. You can take one man's trash to another man but you can't make it drink."

Glancing between Zhao and Bishop, the man was perplexed. "What… are you unwell?"

"You've opened a can of worms, now lie in it."

Before the confused man could answer, Bishop grabbed his collar and hurled him towards a nearby sign advertising a dinosaur lunch special. With one hand on his throat and the other on the knife embedded in his arm, Bishop brought his face close to the writhing man.

"Why does Chang grow impatient? Is Chang working to a deadline?"

With a pained face, the man shook his head. Angrily, Bishop let go of the man's throat and used the heel of his palm to plunge the knife further into the man's arm. The blade sliced the wound open further and jammed into the wooden frame behind him. The man screamed.

"What's Chang's deadline?" Bishop screamed into his face. "Tell me!"

Pupils the size of pinpricks, Mr Shaved Head was

close to losing consciousness. "Friday. Something is happening Friday. That's all I know."

Bishop stood back, his demeanour calm. "Marvellous." He patted the man politely on the head. "You've been an enormous help. Have a nice day."

"That's... that's it?" The man was barely able to speak, the blood loss taking effect. His knees buckled, but he held himself up or the knife would take a greater toll.

Bishop tilted his head. "Oh yes. I don't need anything else." Turning to walk away, he clicked his fingers as if remembering something. "Oh, tell Chang if he follows us to Zhengzhou he'd better watch his back."

With that, Bishop casually walked away. Zhao followed, aghast, her eyes lingering on the man slouched against the wall, crucified. She kept pace, seemingly shocked at Bishop's sudden blasé attitude.

From around the corner, Li came skidding into view. "What happened to the... woah, that guy's nailed to the wall! Did you see the guy nailed to the wall?"

"Come on, time to go, kids." Bishop strode with purpose. "No more rides today." His eyes scanned for any further foes.

Zhao addressed Bishop, concern etched on every feature. "Now what?"

"We'll burn that bridge when we get to it."

She shook her head. "Please stop doing that."

Bishop shrugged. "I'm not sure I can."

Unsure how many assailants had been taken down, nor how many roamed the park, Bishop counted on the park for the next move. As if preordained, an announcement came over the loudspeakers. He turned to Zhao for a translation.

"They're evacuating the park. All emergency exits have just been opened."

Bishop nodded. "They would have locked down the

place after the first explosions in the car park, but after one in the park itself they won't want to be responsible for holding people captive while bombs are exploding. No park manager is going to have that on their conscience."

Li regarded Bishop with awe. "You figured all that out ahead of time? Before we came here?"

"Not all of it. Part of being a field operative is adapting to changes in circumstances, being ready for all eventualities."

"Yeah, but what percentage, though?" Li watched him expectantly.

Bishop grinned. "You don't want to know."

Crowds flowed out of the pavilions and buildings around the park, streaming towards the exits. Most adults had anxiety slapped across their faces, unsure exactly what was transpiring. Parents and guardians held their children tight as they flooded out of the park.

All three MI6 employees headed to the gate furthest away from the car park. They saw no black coats. Within minutes they were trudging through rain-soaked streets free of any tail. Besides the sodden clothes and the weapons they carried, they had no possessions.

"I don't know about you lot," Bishop stretched, "but I could use a nice warm bath."

The Changzhou Shangri-La Hotel was so luxuriously over the top Bishop couldn't help but surrender to the gaudiness of it all. He should have expected nothing less of a hotel shaped like a lotus flower. Not that he saw much of it. He and Zhao slunk in through a rear entrance after Li booked three rooms on his credit card.

Sitting in Li's room in the hotel-issued robes while

their clothes were washed and pressed, Bishop swirled ice in his mini-bar scotch and mused about the last few hours. Kevin Argento knew he was in China and on his tail. Was his text message a greeting or a warning?

Chang was close behind, apparently willing to make any sacrifice and with a deadline of Friday, whatever that signified. Bishop vaguely hoped that some or all of Chang's forces would be sent to Zhengzhou on a wild goose chase after Bishop had dropped the city's name on a whim, but Bishop couldn't rely on that.

There was still no word from The Pope, which, given Chang's sudden appearance, did not bode well for the big American. It was possible he'd made it out and was laying low, but Bishop had to concede it was more hopeful than probable.

Bishop was keen to speak to his superior and work out where to go from here. He'd reported that his impromptu team had performed admirably under harsh circumstances, especially given that one was on a babysitting mission and the other was an IT guy filling in as a driver. On the cautious journey from the dinosaur park, Bishop had taken great care to ensure the two weren't overly traumatised. This wasn't a normal workday for either of them. They'd debriefed well, and by the time they'd reached the hotel, sodden and exhausted, they were in the best mental state possible without extensive psychiatric help.

Washed and rested, they were slowly returning to something resembling a human state. Sitting at the small dining table in Li's room, his two teammates were far cleaner and warmer than when they'd first left the cheesy dinosaur park. Zhao was on her third tiny bottle of spirits from the courtesy bar, a testament to her current state of mind. Seemingly an unseasoned drinker, Li alternated between beer and water, but that didn't prevent his current slurring of words.

"Sho," Li sloshed his beer as he said it, "seeing as I'm on this mission now, who is this guy we're after exactly?"

"Ex-SAS, ex-MI6," Zhao chipped in before Bishop could respond. "Apparently exceptional at both. By all accounts a bit of legend at '6." She turned to Bishop. "Did you ever meet him? Argento, I mean."

Sidestepping the question, Bishop took a sip. "Last I heard the guy was a retiree raising ducks in the Lakes District."

"Right, right." Li gulped some water. "So, how does a pensioner infiltrate a foreign country and manage to take out so many people without being taken down himself? I don't want to sound racist here, but he would stand out in a crowd, right? If he's that washed up, either he's incredibly lucky or has one hell of a guardian angel."

"Like I said, the dude was a legend." Zhao eyed Bishop curiously. Did she know of Bishop's past connection and wonder why he was remaining silent on the topic?

"You think he's trying to commit suicide or something?" Li directed the question to Zhao. "You know, like suicide by cop?"

She shrugged. "Why go all the way to China? It would be far easier to pop a few sleeping pills at home, surely?"

"Then what?" Li shrugged. "Why's he in China killing random dudes?"

"I doubt he's killing at random," Bishop interjected. They both turned to him. "He could kill indiscriminately at home without missing fish and chips. Plus, every minute he stays in China increases his chance of detection." Bishop placed his glass on the table. "There has to be a pattern."

There was that niggling thought again: *Why?* What was Argento trying to achieve? Even if he were completely delusional, there had to be a reason in his mind. Was it related to his son's death? Was this some kind of belated revenge?

Bishop found himself thinking back to the list of bodies Argento had left strewn across the country. More to himself than the other two, he mused out loud, "A newly appointed low-level minister of the Defence committee in the National People's Congress was visiting a farm. Why would he need to visit a farm? It's hardly defence related." When he received no reply, he added, "And why would Argento attack a farm?"

"Maybe he's a militant vegan?"

Zhao tilted her head and ignored Li. "Or maybe it wasn't a farm?" When Bishop nodded, she examined his face. "What are you thinking?"

"What are Defence usually interested in?" Bishop tilted his head.

"Big hats?" Li wasn't keeping up, and seemed lost. "Shiny medals? Marching in formation? Oooh, saluting tanks!"

"Besides that?" The other two stared at Bishop blankly. His mind swirled through the possibilities.

The spell was broken by a knock at the door. All three drew their guns. Carefully, Bishop answered the door, pistol held against it, ready to shoot through the wood. There was no need. It was room service. The waiter quickly put the trays out and scuttled away, tip in hand.

Although he wasn't hungry, Bishop knew he had to eat. He downed his drink as a theory began to form.

Dinner was pleasant. It was the company that made it

so, more than the food. Zhao, of course, had been in charge of room service and over-ordered tremendously. The food was so bland and inoffensive it barely rated as food, but Li and Zhao kept Bishop entertained. Li's charming naiveté was a welcome change in the cynical world of espionage. Zhao, on the other hand, was thoroughly captivating. The more time Bishop spent in her presence, the more confident and commanding she appeared.

Bishop also suspected that the occasional brushes of her foot against the inside of his leg were far less accidental than she claimed. Her furtive glances were also hard to miss. The woman may as well have been using flag semaphores to signal her intent. Bishop had to decide how he felt about that. About Zhao's mood, that was, not flag semaphores.

She was a fellow agent, an extremely attractive and intelligent one, but they were on a mission together and still in hostile territory. The adrenaline rushes associated with brushes with death were well documented, as was the inescapable link between sex and death. After all, the French refer to an orgasm as "la petite mort" or "the little death". If Bishop had time to get all psychological, he knew that being confronted with one's mortality created a significant draw to celebrate life through sex. He knew it well. Intimately well.

His hesitancy wasn't because he was a prude. He'd certainly slept with MI6 staff before. Many times. And their sisters. Vague acquaintances. Girlfriends. Wives.

Since Tessa left, he'd had nothing more than a one-night stand. In fact, if the woman stayed until dawn she was practically a long-term partner. Bishop didn't just fear commitment, he'd developed it into a finely-honed phobia. Was his recent lust for danger a manifestation of that compulsion? He wondered how messed up he'd become after Tessa. His future psychologist bills were going to be massive.

His meandering thoughts were brought into focus by a wayward toe snaking up the inside of his upper thigh. The fact that her toe met resistance so far down gave Zhao a start. She stared at him in shock. The shock soon turned to hunger.

Li, gloriously ignorant of the under-table shenanigans, was trying to sell the other two on the benefits of something called a vocal trance national anthem. Bishop was only half listening. Then Li sloshed his beer into his chocolate mousse.

"Okay, Cowboy." Bishop gently placed his hand over Li's beer and pushed it away. "Time for beddy-byes."

Minutes later Zhao and Bishop carried Li over to his bed. Placing the kid down, Bishop folded a blanket over him and turned off the light. He was sure Li was snoring by the time he shut the door.

In the hallway, Zhao stood patiently, one naked leg noticeably visible out of her robe. With her back arched and her head tilted sideways, she said in a sultry voice, "Care to tuck me in too?"

Lifting his arm in a gentlemanly manner, Bishop grinned impishly. "Why, of course."

As they strode down the luxuriously appointed hallway arm in arm in garish hotel bathrobes, Bishop couldn't miss Zhao rubbing against him. When they reached her door, she used the pass to unlock it without relinquishing her hold on Bishop's arm.

"Take me to bed?" Her voice was suggestive, her face expectant. "I will warn you though, after our slight mishap today, I don't have any pyjamas. I do hope that won't be a problem for you?" Fingers snaking their way through his hair, Zhao leaned forward, panting slowly.

Bishop's voice was low. "I do hope you won't catch a cold."

"Oh, I have some ideas about how to keep me warm, believe me. I can be quite… creative."

"I have no doubt." Bishop extracted his arm from Zhao's and leaned forward to kiss her forehead. "Sleep well, I'll see you in the morning."

Zhao did nothing to hide her shock. "What… you're… you're not coming in?"

Bishop sighed. "I'm as surprised as the next person, but tonight, dear lady, I must politely decline your generous invitation."

He lifted her hand and kissed it before pivoting and walking away. There was no mistaking the devastation on her face.

Taking the lift to the next floor, Bishop tried to work out what had just transpired. Had he actually declined sex? Had that ever occurred before? Zhao was extremely attractive and engaging. And eager. What exactly was the issue? Was it the pressures of the day? The mission? The recent thoughts of Tessa? All of the above?

Still unable to fathom what was going on, he considered calling Zhao and inviting her up. When his hotel room door clicked closed behind him, he flicked the light switch but nothing happened. He tried the nearby bathroom, but the lights refused to work.

Making his way in the darkness, he felt around for the phone to call reception. Before dialling, he sensed another presence in the room. There was a *click*, and a lamp illuminated a person sitting in the corner of the room.

Head tilted to one side, his voice was low and unemotional. "I think you and I are long overdue for a talk, son."

With his pistol aimed at Bishop's heart, Kevin Argento didn't smile.

CHAPTER EIGHT

"How did you find me?" Bishop's trigger finger twitched. The gun in his shoulder holster seemed heavy. He did hate being the only one without their gun out.

"Saw you in park. Suspected they'd send you to come and… have a chat with me. Didn't know if you'd take the job, to be honest." His voice was raspy, tired. Even in the half light, Bishop could see Argento's sunken eyes and unruly beard. This wasn't the sprightly man Bishop remembered. "Then there's the thing at the dinosaur park, good lord." He tutted and shook his head. "Car bombs, explosions. Not exactly stealthy, hmmm? I take it you're the one who nailed the gentleman to a wall?"

Bishop rocked on his heels, suddenly feeling like he was in the principal's office. "I didn't nail anyone to a wall."

"No?"

"No. Absolutely nothing of the sort." Bishop shrugged. "It was a knife."

"Ah, very different." Argento nodded, feigning amusement. The gun in his hand didn't move. "And here you are in the most expensive hotel in the city." He shook his head and frowned. "Did you remember nothing I taught you? This isn't stealth, son. You may as well be running around naked in the People's Congress with fireworks up your arse. A spy's role is to be invisible, not whatever the hell you've been doing. I know you're not good at following orders, but I'm pretty damn sure MI6 didn't order you to explode dinosaurs and close down fun parks."

Bishop crossed his arms. "There were complications."

"There always are with you."

Bishop was keen to change the subject. "You're in my room, you have a gun and you haven't shot me yet. I take it you want something."

"I want you to leave me the hell alone."

Bishop nodded slowly. "Sure, but like you said, I'm not good at following orders."

"Always the smartarse."

"Learnt from the best."

Argento sneered. "What's with the bathrobe? You been getting a massage instead of doing spy work?"

"Got wet. I don't have a change of clothes as my suitcase kind of blew up."

Argento offered no reply. Bishop noticed the plastic-wrapped package hanging on the outside of the wardrobe: no doubt his clothes, having been cleaned and pressed. Now probably wasn't the time to get changed.

The two men glowered at one another. Regardless of what he'd been through, despite his mission, Bishop was glad to see his old mentor alive. Now more than ever he was unsure he could pull the trigger when the moment came. And given how tired the old man appeared, it could be seconds away.

Staring at Argento, Bishop could see he was frazzled, tired and drained, but he didn't appear unhinged. "You're not drunk."

"I am not."

"You're not a fuckup." Bishop tilted his head.

"No, son, I'm not that either." He paused and glanced at the ceiling for a second, then returned his gaze. "Oh, I was there for a while. I reinvented myself." He studied Bishop for a reaction. "Something you're adept at, as well."

No doubt he was referring to the name his mentor had given him years ago. Bishop wasn't keen to go down that particular path of nostalgia. "There are quite a few folks back home who think you're dangerous."

"I love my country."

"Funny way to show it, by starting a war."

Argento slowly shook his head. "I'm not starting a war, son, I'm preventing one." Bishop opened his mouth but Argento raised a finger, silencing him. "Before we get into all that, I need you to do something for me."

Bishop said nothing, just stared. He detected a slight softening in Argento's tone.

The old man swallowed hard. "I need you to do me a favour."

Bishop knew that would have hurt. "If this is about feeding your goldfish, to be honest, I'm not sure I can. I have a lot on. There's my macramé classes, and I've just taken up jazz ballet."

"It's about Tessa, you moron."

That got Bishop's attention. "What about Tessa?"

"I need you to look after her."

"I don't know if she'd be inclined to accept my help." Bishop thought back to the last time he'd seen Tessa at the airport, the dirty expression smeared across her face, the hatred in her eyes. "We aren't exactly on speaking terms."

"Like I give a shit about that." Argento closed his eyes and rubbed his wrinkled face. "I need you to—"

His words were cut short by a sudden rapping at the door. Argento rose out of his chair, pistol trained on Bishop. He slowly closed the gap between them, stopping just shy of striking distance.

In a quiet voice, Argento motioned to the noise. "What's that?"

Bishop shrugged. "It's a door."

Argento issued a heavy sigh. "Don't be an idiot. What's going on with the door?"

"Nothing. It's just standing there."

"Might I remind you I have a short temper and a gun?" Argento frowned. "Find out who it is."

Without moving, Bishop craned his neck and shouted, "Who is it?"

From the other side of the door came the response. "It's Zhao."

Bishop turned to Argento. "It's Zhao."

"Thank you ever so much. Who's Zhao?"

"My partner."

Flicking the gun to the door, Argento said, "Let her in."

Bishop did as instructed. Once he opened the door he saw Zhao. All of Zhao. Standing in the hallway, she wore a flimsy black mesh robe. And nothing else.

Noting the shock on his face, Zhao grinned wickedly. "The gift shop has everything."

She winked and stepped forward, opening the robe to reveal her smooth, naked body. Before Bishop could utter a sound, she stepped forward and thrust her arms around him. Lips locking onto his, she enveloped him in a kiss. "I can't sleep," she purred.

"You'd better come in."

Closing the door behind them, Bishop ushered her into the room. Her sultry demeanour shattered when she saw Argento. To her credit, she didn't scream, just put her hand to her mouth in shock.

Assessing the newcomer, Argento turned to Bishop. "Seems you got over Tessa alright."

Zhao did her best to cover herself, her face flushed.

Bishop frowned. "It was two years ago."

Zhao gawped at Bishop. "Who's Tessa? Wait, who's… is that Argento?"

Argento grabbed Zhao's arm. "Go sit on the chair, please, darlin'."

Situated between Zhao and Bishop, Argento stepped forward, within striking distance. Bishop acted. Laying in a short kidney punch jab with his right, Bishop grasped the hilt of Argento's pistol with his left. Both his hands darted to the gun as Bishop stomped on the side of Argento's knee. The old man cried out. With the gun firmly in Bishop's grasp, and Argento's wrist twisted, Bishop ripped the gun away. He promptly aimed it at Argento's head.

The old man sighed. "That's my technique, you little prick."

Bishop placed the barrel of the gun to Argento's head. "You don't touch her."

Zhao's voice was soft. "Bishop."

Nodding, Bishop stepped away, holding the gun to his old mentor's head. "You're getting slow, old man."

Argento didn't answer. Flicking the gun towards the chair, Bishop motioned him to sit. Once in place, he handed Zhao the gun. Both Zhao and Argento appeared surprised by the action.

Bishop walked over to the dresser and picked up his phone. "I'm going to order an extraction team."

"You're not going to kill me?" Argento crossed his legs.

"Not unless you give me a reason to, old man."

"We have things to talk about."

"We will." Bishop nodded. "While we wait for extraction we'll have plenty of chat time, I assure you. But the sooner I order it in, the sooner we get out of here."

Running through the logistics in his head, Bishop realised he'd have to wake Li up, but he also needed to contact MI6 at the same time.

Addressing Zhao, he said, "Can you get Li and bring him down here?"

A smirk crossed her lips. "In this?" She nodded down to her arms, which were wrapped around herself in an attempt at modesty. The sheer robe certainly didn't leave much to the imagination.

Bishop tilted his head in agreeance. "Fine, I'll get Li. I'll only be a couple of minutes. If he moves, shoot him. If he speaks, shoot him. If he so much as picks his nose, shoot him. Got that?"

"Sure have, boss." She smiled. "Not quite the night I was expecting."

"I'm sure." He gave her a roguish grin. "And best do up your robe. Don't want to give him a heart attack."

Embarrassed, Zhao did just that. Touching his own gun in his shoulder holster, Bishop headed into the hall. There was only one person he wanted to call.

It took several rings, but the answer came through. "I was about to call."

London was seven hours behind; it was early. Paul would have just walked into the office.

The elevator pinged and Bishop stepped in. "I have news."

"I have no doubt." Paul's words were hurried, urgent. "I've read your last report, the one with the dinosaur park."

"Not my finest hour."

"This agent you mention. Zhao…"

"She's a good agent. Reliable, keeps her head when hell breaks loose. She's just the—"

"Bishop." There was a long pause. "We don't know who she is."

The elevator door opened to an empty corridor, but Bishop remained rigidly still. His blood turned to ice in his veins.

"What? The Hong Kong office—"

"Didn't send anyone."

Hitting the button for his floor, Bishop hung up and extracted his pistol. In the decades that passed while the elevator descended, he tried to envisage how it could have happened. He'd sent Zhao's photo and details to MI6 and received a verification message. But he'd been utilising the Chinese phone network. The bastards must have intercepted the messages.

All this time she had been working against him. Was she working with Chang? But she'd killed one of his men. That didn't mean it wasn't part of the ruse. It had certainly cemented her trustworthiness with Bishop. He smashed the hilt of his pistol against the wall of the elevator.

When the door finally opened, Bishop raced down the corridor, then slowed when he reached the door of his hotel room. As quietly as he could, he opened the door. Diving in low, he aimed the gun in all directions, ready for any resistance. He needn't have bothered.

The room was empty. Zhao had taken Argento.

The next two hours passed like a blur as MI6 attempted to trace back the monumental breach that had occurred. Paul never said as much, but Bishop highly suspected there would have been calls for his removal from the mission. He couldn't blame them. He'd only met Zhao, or whatever her name was, the day before, and in all that time Bishop had accepted her identity unchallenged. What sort of spy was he? Yes, he'd submitted the requisite verification check, but instead of the confirmation message coming via the MI6 encrypted app, he'd received a text message. Assuming there'd been an IT issue, he hadn't challenged it. And now his mission was jeopardised because of it. Worse, if Zhao worked for Chinese intelligence the situation would become an international incident at best, a prelude to war at worst.

That brought Bishop's thoughts back to the conversation he'd had with Argento. His former friend had said he was trying to prevent a war, not start one. In Bishop's experience this was not normally achieved by indiscriminately killing citizens of foreign powers. But Argento didn't seemed unhinged. Exhausted, sure, but not unhinged.

Then there were the mysterious defence personnel visiting farms. Where did Zhao fit in? Was she working for the Chinese or some unknown third party, further complicating an already convoluted mission? Bishop knew he didn't have all the pieces to the puzzle. He didn't even have the picture on the box.

One thing Bishop was sure of, however, was what he would do if he ever saw Zhao again. She'd played him for a fool perfectly. In just over twenty-four hours she'd delivered him the most humiliating disgrace in his career. Worse, she'd done it by abducting his former mentor and the father of the woman he still cared for. Then there was the whole potentially starting World War Three thing, but it was mostly about vengeance. The pain he'd inflict upon Zhao would be long and absolute. Having been on both ends of torture, Bishop was most adept at a variety of techniques. Wherever she was,

Bishop hoped Zhao knew the retribution coming her way.

"Want me to call a dentist?"

Bishop looked up. Across the small hotel coffee table, Li sat on the couch staring at him, concern etched across his young face. They both still wore their hotel bathrobes. The young man was tired and hungover, but in the two hours since Zhao had disappeared, Li had shown himself to be an invaluable asset. After Bishop had re-verified his identity, of course.

"What?"

Fighting a hangover, Li attempted to appear reassuring. "You're grinding your teeth so much I was wondering if we should call a dentist before there's nothing left."

Making his best attempt at a smile, Bishop said, "It's the music. What is this?"

"Carl Cox, man. He's a fucking legend. Thought we'd need something drivey to get us going."

"Could you turn it off? Feels like I'm in a nightclub."

Dejected, Li muttered as he worked his phone. "That was kind of the point."

In the ensuing silence, Bishop attempted to gather his thoughts. Unfortunately, revenge would have to wait. They had more immediate concerns. If there was a chance Argento was still in the city, they needed to explore every avenue to get him back. If that failed, they'd have to kill him. MI6 could not allow a former member of their ranks to be interrogated and paraded before the world, no matter how legitimate the Chinese case was. If Bishop had to raze the city to prevent it, that's exactly what he'd do.

"What do we know about Chang?"

Bishop had tasked Li with finding the information, in part, to keep him awake, but mainly to gather further intelligence if it was needed. They still didn't know who Zhao was working for, but smart money would place her with Chang. Bishop recalled Mr Shaved Head saying, "My employer grows impatient". At the time, Bishop took it as a passing comment, but he now remembered Mr Shaved Head watched Zhao as he said it. Was her infiltration not working fast enough? Was that why Chang had acted so rashly when he had his men crash into their car? It seemed plausible.

In response to Bishop's query, Li tapped away on his tablet. "Surprisingly, a lot. Some of it from the Chinese themselves, but most from a data breach we set up a couple of years ago. And some from the NSA, cracked by your mate, The Pope." He sat up. "Right. So, the dude is fifty-four, so he might as well be in an old folks' home."

Bishop chuckled at Li's youthful innocence. He remembered a time when he thought anyone over the age of thirty was positively geriatric. Those days were long gone. He let Li continue.

"Graduated twentieth in his class at Dalian Naval Academy." Li frowned. "That's not very impressive." He continued to read. "Woah, but he was the youngest admiral ever in the People's Liberation Army Navy, at just thirty-six. Ha. That's quite the change of form. I guess it's like all those guys who can say they beat Roger Federer when they were teenagers. The guy ended up smashing it. Uh, anyway, Rear Admiral of North Sea Fleet, incorporating Marines of the 1st Marine Brigade and mechanised forces." Li smiled. "Which I'm going to assume includes Mecha Godzilla."

"Godzilla is Japanese, not Chinese."

Sighing, Li pointed to his face. "Asian. I know the difference. Way to ruin the joke, man." There was no malice in his words; Li was enjoying the playfulness of the discussion. "Then Vice Admiral in the South Seas fleet." Squinting, Li's face creased in confusion. "Then… huh… then nothing for like, twelve months. The next anyone has on him is as one of the heads of Ministry of State Security. How are those two things even related?"

It was a good question. The worlds of espionage and military rarely played well together. With a start, Bishop realised it was the same direction he'd taken. As had Kevin Argento. In fact, Bishop's path from SAS to MI6 had been formulated by Kevin replicating his own. Granted, their journeys were not on the same scale as Chang's, but the similarity couldn't be ignored.

Over the next few hours, Bishop and Li pored over every piece of information they had. There were conference calls and debriefs, reports and assessments. It all boiled down to the same essential elements. They'd had Argento in their grasp and Bishop had lost him.

Both men tried to get a couple of hours of shut-eye before dawn, but in spite of his mounting exhaustion, Bishop couldn't sleep. He wasn't sure if it was guilt or the thirst for vengeance that chased off slumber; probably both.

A little after five, Bishop's phone rang. He answered before the second ring.

"I still think you're an arrogant son of a bitch."

It took several seconds for Bishop's sluggish mind to register the voice. "Pope?"

There was a deep sigh at the end of the line. "Sound like you done fucked up, boy."

Bishop rubbed his face. "Why do you say that?"

"Because if you found Argento with the number I gave you he wouldn't be sitting in the Henglin Police Station, Wujin District of Changzhou, that's why. You couldn't find a man when I gave you his goddamn cell number? What kind of spy are you?"

It seemed The Pope didn't have the full story. Bishop

wasn't about to give it to him. "How did you get the information? Wait, you're safe?"

"Safe enough. For now." The distant sound of a train could be heard in the background. "Since those fuckers burst in and… I've been holed up in one of my hidey holes. Not moving anytime soon. Been leveraging every tap I've got. Finally hit paydirt through Five Eyes. The Canadians had some unrelated surveillance set up and it triggered an alert. They have him, but I don't know for how much longer."

"Why a police station?"

"No idea. That's your job. My guess is they're waiting for extraction and it's the best stronghold they have. Perhaps they've heard of your penchant for mayhem and explosions."

Bishop wasn't going to argue; he had a point. "I owe you."

"That's the understatement of the year." There was a hiss, like the opening of a beer bottle. "And Bishop?"

"Yes?"

"If you cross paths with Chang…"

"I'll let him know the bullet's from you."

"Maybe then we'll be even." The line went dead.

Suddenly alert, Bishop shook Li awake. "Time to get to work. Be ready in fifteen minutes."

He left the groggy kid to wake up and headed into the hallway. Mind reeling, he formulated the foundation of a new plan. He went through their limited weaponry, lack of surveillance equipment, backup or reconnaissance. There would be a lot of winging it. Bishop smelt his armpit. But first, a shower.

After exiting the elevator, he headed towards his room. Bishop knew it contained a beautifully soft bed, but didn't dare contemplate lying down for even a moment. There were far more pressing matters. Before he had opened the door he felt a poke in the centre of his back.

"Hey Bishop. Remember me?"

He turned slowly, and in an instant Bishop under-stood Kevin Argento's request, although there was no time to process the revelation. He had more immediate concerns. Primarily the fact that Tessa Argento stood before him with a gun aimed at his chest.

CHAPTER NINE

"Tessa…"

"Don't you dare Tessa me!"

Her demeanour was angry but restrained, her eyes circled in shadow. She seemed to have had even less sleep than Bishop.

"What would you prefer me to call you? Gertrude? Ruprecht? Gandalf the Grey?"

She clenched her teeth. "Might I remind you I'm holding a gun?"

"No need to remind me. My only question is why?"

"Why?" Tessa snorted. "He went to see you and now he's gone. I've been knocking on your door for an hour. He's not answering his phone. Where's Dad?"

"Would you care to come into my hotel room to discuss this?"

"Oh no, I've fallen for that one before." She scowled. "Where's Dad?"

"That's not an easy question to answer."

"It really is. He's in your room. He's in the bar. He's getting a massage." She poked the barrel of the gun towards his chest. "Where… is… Dad?"

"He's gone."

Her anger evaporated and was replaced with despair. "Gone where?"

"Tessa, I don't know. Someone infiltrated my team and abducted him when I stepped out to call MI6. I don't—"

The right hook caught Bishop by surprise. It was a good one too, sending him staggering backwards. Tessa stepped forward, her eyes watery. Instinctively, Bishop raised his hands defensively. She leapt forward, threw her arms around his neck and sobbed.

His hands hovering above her back, Bishop said, "I'm… I'm not sure what's happening here."

Through tears, Tessa blurted random words. "I… knew… it. He's been taken… by the… Chinese?"

"Yes, but, Tessa." Bishop carefully extracted himself from the embrace. He placed his hands on her shoulders and gazed into her tear-stained eyes. "That's where I'm headed. Where he's being held."

"What?" She wiped away a tear.

"There's a chance, a very small chance, that we might be able to get him out." He looked down at his robe. "I need to shower and change, but we have a location. I can't promise anything, but we're going to try." Bishop gestured to his hotel door. "My clothes are in there. Come in. I'll have a quick shower."

Bishop unlocked the door again and motioned for Tessa to come in. She studied the empty room suspiciously and shook her head. "I'll wait out here."

"Oh please." Bishop sighed. "Like you're a prude. It's nothing you haven't seen a million times."

"I'll wait out here."

Practically pulling Tessa into the room, Bishop shook his head. "I've already lost one Argento today. Come on."

Striding directly to the bathroom, Bishop removed his robe and showered. Over the sound of running water, Bishop shouted, "How did you find him?"

Raising her voice to be heard from the lounge, Tess shouted back. "No thanks to you and your no-fucking-fly flag. I managed to use some pull I had at the Foreign Office to get me unflagged. When I arrived, I sent a message to the phone number Dad said to only ever use in emergencies."

"You said you'd tried every avenue to get hold of him. Didn't you try that one when you were still in England?"

"Of course I did."

"So why did he answer that one?"

"Because it was a picture of me in front of a sign that said, 'Welcome to Beijing'."

"That'd do it."

"Yeah. Imagine how easy your life could have been if you'd worked with me instead of being a total dick."

"I was trying to protect you."

"Like you did Dad? Like you did with Ying Yue?"

There was silence. In the bathroom, Bishop placed both hands on the vanity and assessed himself in the mirror. He hardly recognised the face before him. It had hardened. This mission was changing him. The guilt of Ying Yue's death aged him. He stepped away and into the shower, unable to look himself in the face anymore.

From the other room came a voice, softer than before. "Sorry, that was heartless. I know about it because Dad called The Pope to see if he'd heard from you. He had. He told him the whole story."

"It wasn't me who pulled the trigger, it was a madman named Chang."

"Is he the one who has Dad?"

"I'm not sure. I have a feeling it is."

As quickly as he could, Bishop dried himself. Everything still ached, but now it was a slightly warmer ache. As he towelled himself off he avoided the mirror.

"Who was the person who infiltrated your team?"

Bishop cringed; the memory still stung. Too recent. Too personal. "A woman named Zhao. She faked being a MI6 operative." Tilting his head to the side, a thought struck him. "Huh."

"Huh? Huh what?"

"Just realised. Zhao threw herself at me and I politely declined. Perhaps it was because somehow I knew deep down she wasn't who she said she was."

There was a pause from the other room. "Jesus Christ, Charles. You're equating not having sex with someone to some super-espionage-spider-sense?"

"Possibly?"

"You're unbelievable."

Bishop realised now was probably not the best time to be discussing the subject. He also realised his clothes were out in the other room.

"Tessa? Could you please pass me the dry-cleaning that's hanging on the wardrobe?"

"Uh, sure."

There was a rustling sound, then eventually a hand snaked around the bathroom door. "Here."

Bishop took the clothes with thanks. For a moment, his hand touched hers. In spite of everything, Bishop cherished the intimacy, if only for a fraction of a second. He quickly dressed.

As he pulled on his clothes, Bishop smirked. "I saw you look."

Tessa tutted. "I totally didn't look."

"You had a little look, it's okay."

"I didn't look, Charles."

"You did. A little."

There was a brief silence. "Okay, a tiny peek. There, you happy?"

"I am now."

As urgently as possible, Bishop freshened himself, all the while avoiding the man in the mirror. He knew a shower was nowhere near the same as a good night's sleep—it was akin to slapping a coat of paint over a rusted gate—but it was the best he could do. They had to move.

They raced upstairs to Li's room. When the young guy opened the door, Bishop thought he appeared even more tired than when he'd left. It evaporated in a second when he saw Tessa. Bishop wasn't sure if it was the sudden appearance of a new face or the fact that Tessa was a very attractive woman.

"So, who's…"

Striding into the room, Bishop spoke over his shoulder. "This is Tessa. She's Argento's daughter."

Frowning at the introduction, Tessa followed Bishop into the room. "Hi."

"Oh, hi." Li's head whipped around. "Wait. What? She's… what?"

"She's going to help us." Bishop tried to keep his tone as matter-of-fact as possible, which, given the circumstances, was next to impossible.

"Is this your team?" Tessa addressed Bishop. "Or is there someone else you almost slept with?" Tessa's tone was spear-sharp.

Grinning what he was sure was an insincere smile, Bishop remained mute. He didn't want to get into that particular conversation.

"Is there… uh…" Li scratched the back of his neck and his gaze flicked between the two of them. "Is there some kind of thing going on here? It seems like there's a thing going on."

"All we need to concentrate on is getting Tessa's father out of the police station and out of China."

Tessa sighed, nodding in Bishop's direction. "You should probably know," she huffed, "we dated for a few years."

It was clear Li was struggling to get up to speed. He shook his head several times. "You… you dated your dad?"

Bishop and Tessa stared.

Speaking slowly, Bishop observed Li. "She means me. Tessa and I dated."

Li stepped back, brought his hands to the side of his head and mimed a brain explosion. "What the fuck is going on? What the hell kind of mission is this, man?"

Not entirely sure how to answer, Bishop ignored the question.

"So, like, uh," Li rubbed his eyes and addressed Tessa. "What was your old man doing in China? Why was he killing all those dudes?"

Frustrated, Bishop realised he should have asked Tessa that question well before now. It was the first question he should have asked. Or perhaps the second, after politely asking her to put the gun down. Was it possible she threw him off his game? That was a concern. A subject worthy of examining. Just not now.

"I… I don't know. We only had the briefest time together before he ran off to talk to Charles." Tessa's usual stoicism faltered. "He seemed lucid, fine, better than I'd seen him in ages, to be honest. But… he wouldn't tell me why he was doing what he was doing. He did say…"

Bishop tilted his head. "Said what?"

She turned to face him. "He said you'd understand."

"I would?" He shook his head. "Why on earth would I understand?"

A shrug was his only reply. Her face clouded with concern, and Bishop could sense she didn't want to discuss the subject further.

"Let's get to the planning, shall we?" He stretched his back. "What's our weapon situation?"

He already knew the answer, but was keen to move on.

Li gestured to the bed. "Besides the two in your shoulder holsters, we have mine and three clips of ammunition. Am I counting the one in Tessa's pocket?"

Bishop turned. The outline of Tessa's pistol was barely visible. "Well spotted. We'll make a field agent out of you yet."

"Wait." Tessa's head jutted backward. "He's not a field agent?"

Ignoring the bait, Bishop went on. "Four pistols and a few extra rounds is nowhere near enough to storm a police station. Hell, it's barely enough to storm a haberdasher."

Her eyes narrowed, Tessa assessed Bishop for a moment. "So, it's firepower you want?"

Three minutes later they were in the car park of the Changzhou Shangri-La Hotel. With a theatrical flourish, Tessa opened the boot of a late-model Mercedes-Benz, revealing a veritable stockpile of weaponry. Comms gear, handguns, short and long-barrelled machine guns and some other goodies that made Bishop grin.

"Where did you get these?"

"Dad, obviously. He said he raided one of Chang's weapons stashes."

"Why would the head of the Ministry of State Security need a weapons stash?"

Li piped in. "Maybe because he's not exactly on the

up and up. Because he's not on an officially sanctioned operation. Maybe?"

Nodding, Bishop conceded it made sense. The Chinese are many things, but they don't usually go around summarily executing their own citizens, causing traffic chaos or starting firefights in family fun parks. What exactly was going on?

Bishop pointed at the PF-98 rocket launcher. "How many of those do you have?"

"How many do you need?"

Bishop smiled.

Dawn had had yet to break, and the streets of Changzhou were deserted. From his vantage point in Tessa's car, watching the rear entrance, Bishop hoped the police station was equally uninhabited. The occasional cat trotted down the street, but mostly the soft light of the pre-morning showed a serene stillness.

The plain brick building stood in the centre of the street, seemingly as devoid of life as any other building in the back alleyway. No one seemed to have gone in or out since they took up position. That was good. The quieter the better.

Bishop was still unsure if The Pope's tip-off was accurate, but they were about to bring hell down on this sleepy corner of the world regardless. It was hard for Bishop to know how much of this was for the mission, for Tessa or for himself. As if to convince himself, he repeated in his mind, "for the mission" over and over again like a mantra.

Bishop pressed the button on his comms gear. "Remember folks, we're not here to harm any police, just to get a wayward father and bug out. Minimise casualties. If we accidentally release a criminal or two, that means they'll be busier rounding others up."

"What if one of them is, like, a mass murderer or something?" Li's voice came through crisply. "What if we accidentally release Charles Manson?"

"What if we release a school teacher with three overdue parking tickets? Eye on the prize here, Li. We're trying to prevent Argento being displayed before the world as proof of the UK's officially sanctioned hatred for the Chinese, or whatever their plan is. We fail, this becomes a shooting war, or at the very least, decades of mistrust and economic hell. Make no mistake: if we fuck up, we reshape the world, and not in a good way. Does that put it in perspective?"

Li gulped. "Yeah. Yeah, it does."

"Glad to hear it." Bishop's tone was all business. "You have one minute."

He knew he was being harsh on the kid, but Bishop needed Li's head in the game. Neither Li nor Tessa were trained operatives. Neither were prepared for this, but he needed them. They both supplied an essential element if this was going to work. Which he highly doubted it would. The plan was slapdash at best, but it was all they had.

"Uh, can we also remember we're saving my dad from a firing squad?" Bishop remained silent. Tessa filled the void. "I think that's a pretty freakin' important point too, yeah?"

There was silence. Bishop did his best to remain focused on the worldwide ramifications, as the personal ones were just too personal. Focusing on the political implications allowed him to retain an air of detachment, to help him delude himself that this was just another assignment. But it wasn't. It never would be.

Seeing Tessa again had really rammed it home. All the

professional detachment in the world did nothing to prevent his heart beating faster every time he saw her face. Even when she was screaming at him, or held a gun on him, for that matter, it made no difference. He still longed for her touch, to hear her soft voice, to be cradled in her arms.

What would Kevin Argento make of all that? The ex-agent in him would abhor Bishop's detestable unprofessionalism. The father would likely take a slug at him, in much the same way his daughter had. Bishop and Argento's seemingly unbreakable bond had disintegrated as soon as he'd found out about his relationship with Tessa. Years of trust and friendship had dissolved the instant Bishop told Argento he loved his daughter. The disloyalty was too great, the betrayal so complete.

Bishop offered no reply to Tessa's terse message. Partly because if she was angry with him, she could use it. It would help centre her attention and provide laser sharp focus. Then again, it could also be that Bishop was a coward who was avoiding a confrontation. It was hard to tell sometimes.

"Twenty seconds."

"Charles." Tessa's voice seemed paper thin, frail. "I'm not sure I can…"

"Tessa, I'm saying this without a word of a lie. You're the strongest woman I've ever known. You can do this. In twenty minutes, it will all be over. We'll go have a beer with your dad and he can get back to hating my guts. But before then…" Bishop peered through the sight. "You have to pull the trigger. In five."

"Charles."

"Four."

"I don't think…"

"Three."

"Wait."

"Two."

"Charles, please."

"One. Pull the damn trigger, Tessa. Now!"

She did. Dawn came early to Changzhou. The world burned.

CHAPTER TEN

The first explosion hit the electricity transformer substation half a block from the police station. The resultant fireball lit up the sky like a new sun. Nestled in the alley behind the police station, Bishop shielded his eyes from the intense brightness of the explosion.

The next blast was mild by comparison. It hardly registered amid the reverberations of the first. It took out the front door of a dog grooming salon. Not exactly a significant target, but it served a strategic purpose.

The third was slightly more spectacular. A group of three luxury cars, two Porsches and a Lamborghini, were parked in front of a fancy hotel. It was the same the world over: park the most beautiful cars in front of the hotel to provide a greater sense of opulence. The last of the 120 mm unguided anti-tank rockets was launched from the PF-98 and slammed into the cars. There was a reason the Chinese called the launcher the "Queen Bee". The explosion was similar to the first.

In the back alley, all was dark. All the lights were out as far as Bishop could see, police station included. With *thump*, a flaming side mirror landed on top of the hood of Bishop's car.

As he watched the red plastic melt, Bishop said, "Nice shootin', Tessa. Now get out of there."

Heavy panting came through the comms system. "Way ahead of you."

Her mission complete, Tessa's job was to run away as fast as possible and be nowhere near the entrance to the police station.

"Did you douse it?"

Panting, Tessa responded, "Yep. Don't want you to have to break me out of the station next."

They'd found undiluted hydrogen peroxide in a cleaning cupboard of the hotel. Tessa had been tasked with ditching the PF-98 and pouring the liquid all over it. The bleach would destroy all fingerprints, oxidising the surface to burn all traces of anyone who had handled it. The last thing they wanted was for Tessa to be caught walking the streets with a rocket launcher slung over her shoulder. Even her radiant smile wouldn't get her out of that one.

Bishop was glad her role was done. Her aim had been three for three. Not bad for someone who hadn't been sure she'd be able to pull the trigger.

The next part of the plan, Bishop was less sure of. He tapped the talk button. "You ready?"

"Already on my way in." Li kept the line open. Through the earpiece, Bishop could hear Li play his part. The door to the police station swung open and he yelled in Mandarin. Bishop didn't understand the words, but knew the English version of it. "Quickly, there's terrorists! They just blew up some cars and the electricity thing." Li was adamant his story would gain credibility if he didn't use the word "transformer". "They're headed that way, in a red BMW SUV." He would now be pointing away from

Bishop's position. "You can still catch them if you go now!"

In the dark station, there would already be confusion. They would be panicked and directionless. It would be the last thing they'd expected on a quiet Tuesday morning. Li's panicked shouts would provide a chance for them to focus their nervous energy. To move. To act.

The subsequent overlapping authoritative shouts seemed to support that theory. In the next two minutes, orders were barked and Bishop recognised the sound of weapons being distributed. The sound of stomping feet and doors slamming was followed by relative silence.

Li spoke in a low voice. "Five gone. Two left."

"Thirty seconds," Bishop clicked his watch, "and mark."

Opening the car door, Bishop headed to the boot and extracted a rocket launcher of his own.

A rattling metallic sound surprised him. He turned to see a roller door covered in stickers slide up. A sleepy middle-aged man in shorts and t-shirt stared at Bishop, wide-eyed. Bishop hoisted the PF-98 onto his shoulder and slowly shook his head. The shopkeeper nodded, stepped back and quietly slid down the roller door.

First checking his watch, Bishop used the launcher's sight to aim at the rear door of the police station. After watching the seconds count down, he said, "Incoming."

Bishop pulled the trigger. Pushed back by the force of the recoil, he watched a trail of smoke snake its way through the chilly morning air. The explosion lit up the darkened alleyway. Tossing the Queen Bee in the back of the car, he extracted a Heckler & Koch MP5 and slammed the boot shut.

Sprinting towards the entrance, Bishop heard Li issue angry shouts, no doubt along the lines of, "Don't move or I'll shoot". Bishop leapt through the charred and smouldering doorway, splinters of wood and masonry scattered on the ground.

The station was pitch black. Bishop clicked on the torch attached to the barrel of the submachine gun. The shaft of light created eerie shadows as it illuminated the smoky confines of the station.

Like most police stations the world over, logic dictated that the cells be positioned near the back, away from the general public entrance and close to the rear exit for trouble-free prisoner exchange. It took mere moments for Bishop to find the cells. There were no other police. Li must have them all pinned down at reception.

There were three darkened cells. Fewer than Bishop had expected. Two were empty. The third held the prize.

Bishop shone the torch at him. "I'm Luke Skywalker, I'm here to rescue you."

Argento shielded his eyes from the bright light. "You're a damn fool."

"You're meant to say I'm a little short to be a Stormtrooper. Honestly, I don't know why I bother."

Argento crossed his arms and scowled. "I distinctly remember teaching you stealth, son. What do you think you're doing?"

"We'll have enough time for the grovelling gratitude later." Bishop aimed his weapon at the lock. "For now, let's get you out of here."

Firing three rapid rounds, Bishop made short work of the lock and the cell door swung open. Despite his gruffness, Argento was on his feet and following his rescuer without a word of protest. He didn't want to hang around the police cells any more than Bishop did. The old mentor and student charged through the empty station.

Nearing the blown-out exit, a figure stepped forward, cutting them off. Without missing a step Argento picked up a hefty stapler and readied himself for attack.

Pushing Argento's arm down, Bishop spoke quietly. "It's okay. He's with me."

Li beamed. "Hey hey, nutsacks."

Argento glared wide-eyed at Bishop. "*He's* with you?"

Bishop ignored the bait. "All good?"

"Yep." Li seemed pleased with himself. "The two remaining cops are handcuffed to a desk. They'll be fine, only damage will be to their pride. As an added bonus, I found the comms room. No backup power there, no CCTV; we're clean."

"Good work." Bishop jerked his head towards the door. "Let's go."

The trio leapt out the shattered rear entrance. Dawn was slowly breaking and a muted light illuminated the empty street. Well, almost empty. Standing near the car was a figure, her bare shapely legs protruding from beneath her trench coat. She'd made her way around the block to the rendezvous point. Bishop had no desire for the police to pick Tessa up wandering the streets and find out who she was related to. He couldn't bear anyone laying a hand on her.

The soft morning light gave her an ethereal glow. There was no doubt about it, the woman was stunning.

When Argento reached the car, Tessa threw her arms around the big man and buried her head in his shoulder.

With a whimper, she whispered, "You're safe."

"Not yet, he's not." Bishop tossed the keys to Li. "You drive. Tessa, you're in the passenger seat. Kevin, back seat with me."

Making her way around the car, Tessa stopped in front of Bishop. "Thank you, Charles."

"My pleasure."

"No." She placed a hand on his cheek. "Thank you." Her gaze was firm but gentle. In an instant Bishop was reminded of endless nights gazing into her green eyes and becoming lost in them, their bodies tangled as one. It was a beautiful memory, painful to recall.

Li and Tessa took their assigned positions and Argento nodded, knowing exactly what Bishop had in mind. With the two of them in the back seat, they could coordinate efforts if bullets started flying. In preparation, Bishop opened the boot, extracting pistols and boxes of ammunition.

That's when he heard the squeal of tyres. He turned to see a white van careening towards them. This wasn't someone out for a casual pre-dawn drive. Whoever was in the van was after them.

The white van bounced along the narrow road at breakneck speed and would be on them in seconds. In an instant Bishop calculated the time it would take him to run around the car, get in and take off. They wouldn't make it. And even if he did, they would have someone right on their tail. He had to buy them time.

There was only one thing to do.

He slammed down the boot and shouted to Li. "Go now, that's an order."

Without waiting for a response, Bishop sprinted towards the oncoming van to reinforce the fact that there would be no debate. To his credit, Li did as he was told. He floored it. Bishop smiled at the screech of tyres. At least she'd be safe.

Bishop slowed, and stood alone in the centre of the street, a pistol in each hand. The day broke over the horizon behind him, giving the scene a spectral feel. The van hurtled forward. There was no way around him: they'd have to stop or mow him down. Either option would allow the others to get away.

The van was almost upon him. He tossed the guns aside and placed his hands on his head, smiling. The roar of the engine enveloped him, the headlights blinding.

At the last second the van skidded, lurched forward and slammed backwards, mere centimetres from Bishop's chest. The engine ticked away for what seemed like hours. The glare of the headlights made it impossible for Bishop to see into the cabin.

Two figures emerged, one from either side of the vehicle, their boots echoing around the silent street.

Shielding his eyes, Bishop put on his most affable expression. "Oh, hey. I'm a bit disoriented. Can either of you point me towards Piccadilly Circus? I fear I'm terribly lost."

The two figures didn't appear amused. Chang and Zhao aimed their weapons at Bishop.

The first five minutes were a flurry of punches. And the next five. Then things got really nasty.

With both wrists handcuffed to the interior roof of the van, Bishop couldn't put up much of a fight. His bare feet were handcuffed too—or perhaps they were called feetcuffs, Bishop wasn't sure. He earned extra punches when he asked. When Chang's henchman grew weary, the muscle-headed creep gave his wrists a shake and went to the front of the van to recuperate. Bishop couldn't bring himself to feel sorry for him.

Bishop turned to Chang. "Just so you know, I'm giving this place a terrible review on Trip Advisor."

The older man barely raised a condescending grimace. The van Chang and his two assailants had picked Bishop up in wasn't large. Bishop could kick the driver's seat if he wanted to—if he had the energy. His battered form was so drained he could hardly stand. Chang and Zhao stood at the rear of the van, doing their best to appear indifferent to the beating. The henchman was short and built like a boulder, pure muscle and wrath. He also doubled as a driver: he'd been the one to drive the van to the empty industrial car park where they now were.

Bishop ground his bare feet into the floor of the van, forcing himself to remain present and to retain his wits. He was still alive, able to touch. The sensation of the grit against his skin grounded him, re-energised his senses.

Chang and Zhao spoke in hushed tones. The words were unfamiliar, but their demeanour wasn't. There was an intimacy in their exchange, not sexual—Chang could be her father—but familial. The two were close. Their words intermingled, one's short sentences were completed by the other, quick quips were rewarded with smirks, as if acknowledging old in-jokes. Bishop wondered if he could use their familiarity to his advantage.

"She's very good at what she does." He nodded towards her. "Zhao, or whatever her name is. She had us fooled from minute one. You've taught her well. You must be very proud of your creation."

Chang sighed. "You make me sound like Dr Frankenstein and she the monster."

Bishop's handcuffs rattled as he pointed to his collar. "It's the bolts on the neck."

Throughout their exchange Zhao remained silent. Bishop was unsure if it was because she was acceding to her superior, embarrassed at having duped him so thoroughly or perhaps she arrogantly believed she was above such conversations. It was hard to tell.

Tilting his head at his captor, Bishop smiled. "How was your flight, Chang?"

The head of State Security baulked. "How was my... how on earth did you know I'd been on a flight?"

It was poor form for Chang to have confirmed Bishop's assumption so freely, but Bishop let it slide. "The van still has the cardboard advice hanging from the rear-view mirror, meaning it's a hire. There are bags in the front seat with tags on the handles. And finally, the stain on your collar is black bean sauce from the Hainan first-class selection."

Bishop put on his best smug façade. The last point was designed to annoy the ex-admiral, as it was a complete fabrication, but it seemed to have the desired effect.

"Don't tell me you flew all the way to Zhengzhou?" On seeing Chang's annoyance, Bishop burst out laughing. "Oh, that's precious! I said it as a joke to your guy as I was crucifying him. Too funny." Bishop shook his head in mock amusement. "Tell me, were you on your way to pick Argento up from the police station when he was sprung?" Again, Chang's face was like a brightly lit billboard, confirming Bishop's assumptions. "My, that must be frightfully annoying."

"Enough!" Chang clenched his fists, irritated.

He spoke rapidly to Bishop's torturer, who went to sit in the driver's seat. Seemingly a man of few words, the Brute sat silently, leaving Chang and Zhao to their interrogation.

"Now Yang has softened you up, you can provide some answers." Chang leaned forward and sneered. "Who do you work for?"

"Avon." Bishop's tone was matter-of-fact.

"What?"

"I know, I know, everyone says I should move over to Mary Kay, but I've invested so much it would be like starting from scratch, and I don't know if I'm ready for that type of transition, you know?"

Chang stared at Bishop for the longest time, his face a

melange of frustration, annoyance and bewilderment. "Are you really that stupid?"

"I don't know," Bishop tilted his head, "are you? Your offsider there infiltrated my group by impersonating an MI6 operative. We spoke of MI6. You know who I work for, so perhaps we could skip the boring exposition parts and get to the meat of the matter."

"Which is?"

Bishop squinted. "How are you off for lipsticks?"

The slap was brutish and efficient. Bishop's head snapped around. He would have fallen if not for the handcuffs.

Bishop tasted the blood trickling from his lip. "What about blush? With your complexion, I'd really recommend—"

The punch to the gut knocked the wind out of him, and for several seconds he struggled for air. It was a shame, it really took the fun out of annoying Chang. The man was quick to temper, far too easy to rile. There was an unhinged nature to him. Bishop's mind raced, trying to find ways to use it to his advantage, but they all circled back to the same unequivocal conclusion: he was screwed.

At least his capture had served a purpose. The fact he remained alive was evidence enough that his diversionary tactic had been successful. It appeared the others had managed to make it out. There would be no need to interrogate Bishop otherwise. If Chang's goons had Argento, Bishop would have a hole in his forehead and be rotting in a ditch somewhere. Chang needed information, that meant the others were free. She was free.

Bishop knew he would not share their fate. The only three individuals who could potentially aid him had no idea where he was. There would be no miraculous rescue, no daring escape. Bishop's destiny was as plain as it would be brief.

Yet, even in the face of all that, Bishop couldn't combat years of training. He still planned. Still schemed. It was futile, but Bishop couldn't help himself. If he was to go down, he'd go down swinging. His mind raced.

The van was a new addition. The day before, there had been four SUVs. In Bishop's estimation, three had been written off in the traffic skirmish. Yet here he was in a van. Perhaps the one remaining black SUV was scouring the streets for Argento, Li and Tessa. Bishop hoped he'd given them a sufficient enough head start. It was possible the van was all Chang had been able to hire on short notice. Then there was the question of why Bishop was there at all.

"Why a van?" Bishop did his best to appear off-the-cuff. Which took quite an effort, given said cuffs were chained to the ceiling of the van.

"What?" Chang was visibly annoyed.

"I'm wondering why a van, you know? Why not interrogate me in a regular facility? Or the police station, for that matter?"

"You're not entirely popular there, or don't you remember blowing it up?" It was the first time Zhao had addressed him since he'd entered the van.

"Yes, but," Bishop waggled his finger, "that's not it. You see, if you had apprehended the perpetrator of the attack, and of course I admit to doing no such thing, then you'd have all the security you could eat. But instead we're in this off-the-shelf budget rental van. Therefore, I'm left wondering why a van? Hmm? Did you need a quiet place for your cry-wanking?"

"Do you have a point besides being vulgar?" Chang seemed close to losing his temper again.

"The van, the handcuffs, they were intended for

Argento, right? If so, why weren't you interrogating him at the police station?" Bishop tilted his head. "Unless whatever you thought you were going to extract from Argento wasn't for everyone to hear. Hence—" Bishop waved his hands around the interior of the van.

That's why Argento was untouched when Bishop had arrived at the station. He hadn't been interrogated. Yet. Chang wanted to conduct his questioning away from other departments. The van was the perfect place. It also made disposing of the body far easier.

"Whatever this is," Bishop shook his handcuffs, "it isn't sanctioned. In fact, I'm guessing your whole damn operation is off the books. Why have weapons stashes around the country? If this was legitimate you wouldn't need black SUVs roaming the countryside, would you? You'd have police, the army, air force and dog catchers coming down on us faster than you could say little red book. But you don't, do you? *You* were the one who suppressed the fact that it was Argento who'd been photographed at the farm because you wanted him for yourself. And why leave Argento languishing in a cell overnight? That seems slapdash, unless it was the most secure place you could get with limited influence and funding. No," Bishop sniffed, "you've got your own agenda and it certainly doesn't have a governmental stamp of approval, at least not yet. I wonder who *you're* working for, Chang?"

Throughout his rant, Bishop scrutinised Chang's face. He wasn't terribly good at concealing his surprise and emotion. There were cracks, some Grand Canyon-wide, in his features. The man was a walking billboard.

Chang's manner put Bishop on edge. There was an ever-present danger to the man. He was like a crouched lion, ready to tear you to shreds at a moment's notice.

"Enough babble." With a tilted head, Chang

attempted to appear charming. He failed miserably. "Where is it?"

"Where's what?"

Chang shot Bishop a solid punch to the solar plexus. It was a good jab, efficient. It took the wind out of his sails for a few seconds.

The older man's face reddened. "Where is *it*?"

Finally, they got to the point. Bishop was amazed it had taken so long, given that his team could be speeding in any direction. He also recalled what Mr Shaved Head had said at the dinosaur park—something was going down on Friday. Chang was on the clock, and the rapidly approaching deadline was making him desperate.

Bishop wondered how long he could hold out. Not long, based on the brutality of their warm-up tactics. He just had to buy the others enough time to get as far away from Chang as possible.

Bishop was ready to begin. "We're referring to Argento as an it, now, are we?"

Chang raised his hand to strike but appeared to think better of it. Brutality was more effective when used sparingly. He leaned in menacingly. "Where's the case?"

Bishop didn't immediately reply. For several seconds, he wondered if Chang was referring to Argento as a case. But that didn't make sense. "What case?" The agitation on Chang's face was obvious. He thought Bishop was playing dumb. He wasn't. He really was dumb. "No really, what case?"

Chang drew back his hand to slap Bishop, but Zhao softly placed her hand over the older man's arm to stop him.

She watched Bishop as she spoke to her superior. "In all our time together, he never once mentioned the case. He may know nothing of it."

What was the case? More importantly, what was

inside the case, and why was Chang so interested in it? All this time Bishop had believed Argento was their prize, but was there something else at play here? What was Bishop missing?

Bishop's whole mission dynamic had changed. He was glad he'd disregarded his initial assignment parameters; everything was far muddier and more complex than it had seemed at Vauxhall Cross. This wasn't a wet job. This didn't require a blunt instrument. There was far more going on.

When it all boiled down to it, Bishop only had one mission now: stop Chang.

A garbled message came through the radio at the front of the van. Yang, the sometimes torturer, sometimes driver, had an urgent conversation with Chang. The head of State Security turned slowly to Bishop, his face twisted in a sadistic expression.

"Your friends have been spotted on a traffic camera." He leaned in so Bishop could witness his glee up close. "Shall we go find them? I look forward to watching your face when you see them tortured and killed due to your ineptitude. Would you like that, *Bishop*?" He spat his name like venom.

The bastard was going to intercept Bishop's team. He was going to lay a hand on Tessa. Bishop couldn't allow it. The MI6 agent's jaw clenched. He closed his eyes and steadied himself.

Chang assessed Bishop, from his bare feet to his matted hair. "You know something, Bishop? Before the day is out you'll be begging me for your life."

Bishop grinned a bloody smile. "You first, Chang. You first."

Chang clicked his fingers. Yang started the engine and within seconds the van was heading out of the industrial car park. In a few quick turns it was on a highway. It was early morning, and the traffic was heavy on the other side of the highway, presumably meaning the van was headed away from the city.

The van swerved around a slow-moving tractor too quickly, sending Chang and Zhao stumbling against the rear of the van. This was Bishop's one chance. With his hands grasping the handcuffs on the roof of the van, Bishop's legs shot out towards Yang in the driver's seat. Hoisting his manacled feet over the driver's head, Bishop looped the chain of the handcuffs around the driver's neck and pulled. With the balls of his feet pressed firmly on the back of the headrest, he pushed with everything he had. Yang's hands left the wheel as he clawed at the chain strangling the life from him.

Chang lunged forward, hitting Bishop's legs to dislodge them, but they held true like they were set in concrete. Despite repeated thumps of his fists, Chang couldn't remove Bishop's feet. In the reflection in the rear-view mirror, Bishop saw Yang's face turning purple.

Gritting his teeth, Bishop heaved and sprung his feet off the headrest and heard a satisfying crack from the front of the vehicle. Yang's neck had snapped. Realising that the van was veering off the road, Chang scrambled towards the steering wheel.

As the van careened across the highway towards oncoming traffic, Chang struggled to correct their course.

Horrified, Zhao turned to Bishop. "You've killed us all!"

Looking at Chang at the front of the van and the rapidly approaching red truck, Bishop smiled and said, "Mission accomplished."

Bishop kept smiling right up until they crashed.

CHAPTER ELEVEN

Chang wrenched the wheel as the truck before them swerved to avoid the collision. The big lorry careened off the road into an embankment, and the out-of-control van tore forward into oncoming traffic. Handcuffed to the roof, Bishop was under no illusions about his fate. He just hoped it would be quick.

With no foot on the accelerator, the van slowed. But not enough. A green Ford saw the oncoming van and slammed on the brakes, but too late. Neither vehicle was at full speed, but it mattered little. The crash was still awful.

The two solid masses colliding produced a deafening cacophony of sound. Solid metal folded like paper as fragments of plastic and glass flew in all directions.

The front of the van crumpled and Chang was launched through the front windscreen. Zhao's untethered body flew forward and smashed sideways into the back of the driver and passenger seats. Bishop, shackled to the roof, clung to the chains, trying not to lose his hands. The impact threw him upward into the roof and everything went black.

When Bishop came to, his ears rung and his wrists felt like they were on fire. He could hear the hiss of escaping steam and the death-rattle clank of a dying engine. The impact had been far slower than it could have been, but it was still brutal.

The entire front of the van had crumpled into the Ford, which seemed to have sustained little damage thanks to the reduced speed of the crash. The lone driver of the other vehicle blinked at Bishop in disbelief. Her morning commute had taken a dramatically violent turn. She was in shock, but her airbags had deployed and she seemed outwardly unscathed.

The driver's seat of the van had become dislodged in the accident and lay facing upwards on the floor of the van. Ignoring the shouts and screams from outside, Bishop edged his feet towards the corpse of his torturer. Yang's legs were wedged in the crumpled mess of the front of the van. His upper body was mainly intact, but the impact had propelled his head forward, causing significant damage. There wasn't a lot of blood from the wounds, given that his heart had stopped before the collision.

Ignoring the bloodied and ripped flesh of his wrists, Bishop attempted to draw the driver closer. The lifeless body was limp and heavy, hampering Bishop's efforts. Shouts from the rear of the van told him he had limited time. He couldn't wait for assistance from a concerned rescuer; they might leave him chained up, thinking he was handcuffed to the roof for a good reason.

Managing to loop his manacled feet around Yang's arm, Bishop pulled. The strain on his bloody ankles and wrists screamed for respite, but there was no time for such luxuries. With a heave, Bishop dragged Yang's body towards him. It was only after the stench hit his nose that

Bishop realised the upper body moved so freely because it was now detached from the lower half.

Fighting nausea, Bishop crept his foot into the top pocket on Yang's shirt. His toes hit metal and Bishop felt a wash of relief. But he was far from safe. Banging could be heard at the rear of the van. Someone was trying to get in. Bishop used his toes to drag the key out of the pocket. Just as it reached the top of the pocket, the key slipped down Yang's shirt and away. If it slid all the way down, it would be beyond his reach. A panicked stamp of his foot halted the key's escape just in time. Bishop blew out a sigh of relief.

Slowly, he scrunched his toes and brought his feet skyward. Though his wrists screamed in pain, he hefted his legs higher until his feet met his hands. With tongue hanging out the side of his mouth, his shaking fingers plucked the key from between his scrunched toes. *Thank you, core strength.*

Ensuring he didn't lose momentum, Bishop quickly unlocked the cuffs and collapsed to the floor of the van, then freed his feet. Taking the time to extract Yang's pistol from its holster and tucking it in behind his back, Bishop crawled to Zhao's prone body, which lay motionless on the floor. He checked for a pulse. She was alive. Bishop moved his other hand to her slender neck. She'd earned it. The bitch had played him for a fool and fully deserved her fate. With teeth clenched, he squeezed.

Seconds later, Bishop unlocked the van's rear doors. The assembled morning commuters stepped back when they saw Bishop's battered body. Or perhaps it was his crazed look of determination. Planting his bare feet onto the road, he staggered away, searching for an escape vehicle.

A heavyset male in his late twenties, dressed in overalls, stepped forward. Behind him was a van covered in

PVC pipes and ladders: a plumber. The man shouted as he pointed to the back of the van. Bishop took his words to be the Chinese equivalent of "Oi, what the fuck, mate?"

Nodding politely, Bishop aimed the gun in his direction. The plumber backed away, flinging his hands in the air, and replied in a calm, conciliatory tone. The guy was brave, Bishop had to give him that. He saw a bloodied, barefooted madman leaving two bodies in the back of a van and bravely stepped in. But Bishop had a mission to complete.

The good Samaritan plumber was about to scurry away when Bishop tutted and shook his head. It was unfortunate, but the plumber's van was at the head of the traffic jam; the only vehicle able to drive away. They keys were in the plumber's hand. Bishop made apologetic gestures as he relieved the plumber of his keyring. Grabbing what he needed from the crashed van, Bishop made his way to the plumber's vehicle.

As he started the van, Bishop formulated what he would do next. It would get ugly, and there would surely be casualties along the way. Bishop slotted the van into gear, gripped the steering wheel tightly and stamped the accelerator to the floor.

He had somewhere to be.

There was only one derelict road in and out of the city. Bishop didn't even know if it could be considered a city. Could a city be a city if no one lived there? Long Cheng was one of China's infamous uninhabited cities, built in the middle of nowhere in the fervour of a construction boom, with no regard as to whether it was needed or not.

The midday sun beat down on the bright, silent city.

Bishop had seen it when he, Li and Zhao were driving to find Argento. Before they blew up the police station, Bishop had told the others that the derelict city was to be their fallback. If they made it out of Changzhou, they would hide out in the abandoned city for a day or two before moving on once the heat died down. Where better to hide out than somewhere there wasn't another soul for kilometres? Somewhere with all the hiding places you could imagine?

Bishop hoped the others had made it this far. When Chang received the alert about Bishop's team having been spotted, he'd managed to stop the madman, but he didn't know if it was enough. He had no idea if anyone else could have taken down Tessa and the others. Fear gripped his chest: what if he found the city truly abandoned?

As the plumber's van reached the final incline into the silent city the wheels lost traction on the makeshift gravel road. Dropping it into a lower gear, Bishop kept his speed consistent. After several more slips, the van surged onto perfectly level and smooth asphalt. The difference was remarkable. From the bumpy, unkept surface of the lone access road to the marble-smooth, flawlessly laid boulevard in the blink of an eye.

As he drove, Bishop had to remind himself he wasn't in an actual city. Pristine multi-storey buildings towered over precisely laid-out streets, with signs and traffic lights servicing no one. There was a shopping mall, apartment buildings, parks and bus stops. The only thing the city didn't have was any signs of life. It was like a scene from a post-apocalyptic movie.

Unfortunately, in their haste, Bishop's team hadn't decided exactly where in the abandoned city they should meet. It was possible Bishop could drive around all day without finding his team. He briefly considered writing,

"Hey, it's Bishop!" on the side of the van but thought it slightly less stealthy than he needed to be.

Deciding to concentrate on the centre square, Bishop drove around it several times, scrutinising the buildings for any movement. The city square, with its empty water fountain, was surrounded by municipal buildings, the front entrance of an incomplete shopping mall and a cinema, as well as several apartment buildings. After ten minutes of driving fruitlessly in circles around the same dull square, Bishop contemplated where else in the city he could forage for his team.

As he turned for one final lap, the driver's side mirror exploded in a shower of plastic and glass. Bishop swore. Hitting the brakes, he skidded to a halt. Gambling that the shot had been fired by his people and not the opposition, Bishop turned off the engine and exited the van with his hands on his head.

Blinking into the sun, he tried to see where the sniper had struck from. There were so many windows, it could have been anywhere.

Fifty metres away, a woman stepped into the centre of the road. Not just any woman. Dressed all in black, she balanced a sniper's rifle on her hip and a devilish grin on her lips.

Bishop walked forward and shouted, "You missed."

"No, I didn't." Tessa gave a cheeky smirk. "You're still breathing."

"Have I done something wrong?"

"More than you could possibly imagine."

"I'm talking recently."

"I'm not."

When Bishop finally drew close to Tessa, she gave him a self-satisfied smirk. "You're a plumber now?"

"You're a sniper now?"

Rolling her eyes, she pointed to the van. "Get that

thing off the street. There's an underground car park over there beneath the Town Hall. We're in the offices next door. I'll meet you there." About to move away, Tessa seemed to change her mind. She turned to face Bishop. "What you did was incredibly stupid."

"I was trying to—"

Bishop stopped talking when she stepped forward and kissed him on the cheek. "Thank you for being stupid."

She trotted off without waiting for a reply, leaving Bishop standing in the middle of the street, bemused.

Bishop parked in the spacious but empty underground car park, and noticed Tessa standing by the stairs. With the sniper's rifle slung on her back and a hand on one hip, she appeared every bit the warrior queen.

The kiss on the cheek may have been a spontaneous show of appreciation, but he doubted it. Tessa rarely did things spontaneously. As he walked closer, he noticed that her eyes never left his. Her red lips sparkled in the muted neon lighting. In fact, if he wasn't mistaken, the lipstick appeared freshly applied.

Bishop tilted his head. "I appreciate you not shooting at me this time."

Tessa shrugged. "The day is early and my armaments many."

"How's your father?"

"Surprisingly fine after the stint in the police cells. He thinks they were holding off on him until Chang arrived."

Letting out a chuckle, Bishop smirked. "I think he may be onto something there."

Opening the door to the stairwell, far brighter lights hit Bishop and he squinted.

Tessa grabbed his arm and stopped him. Her delicate fingers touched the bloody rings around his wrists. "My god, Charles. What did they do to you?"

"Nothing I didn't pay back tenfold."

"I've got a medi kit in the car. Come on."

She led him back into the car park and over to the car they'd escaped in. Tessa delicately applied antiseptic cream and bandages to the weeping sores and tended to his many cuts. When she finished, she regarded him as if he were a stranger.

She shook her head. "I can't… I find it difficult to…"

Bishop placed his hand on her cheek. "What is it?"

"I just… it's hard to reconcile what you do for a living with the man I once knew. The kind, loving man who I spent years beside. It's not easy, that's all."

"It will all be over soon."

"I don't know if I want it to be."

Without waiting for a reply, Tessa stood up and walked to the stairs. Bishop followed at a more leisurely pace. He couldn't spend time determining what her statement meant. There were far more imposing and deadly matters to focus on.

He made it upstairs to the conference room, but it was a struggle. Everything hurt. But he couldn't let the team see it. He had to forge through. Bishop was their only chance, they had to believe in him.

Opening the door, he saw the team sitting around an ugly grey conference table. Li and Argento poked around what appeared to be a service station feast. Empty chocolate and chip packets were surrounded by cans of drink and overflowing shopping bags.

Both men stood to greet Bishop. Li ran up and gave Bishop a hug, then patted him on the shoulder, apparently unable to speak. Argento gave him a curt nod, giving away nothing. There was no warmth in his greeting. The others seemed to sense the tension too.

Tessa reminded Li it was his watch, and sent him several floors up to keep an eye out for any sign of approach. From that crow's nest position, she'd apparently spotted Bishop twenty minutes before she'd made her presence known. Why she'd let Bishop drive around so long, he could only speculate. He suspected it might have something to do with her recent experience at Heathrow.

Bishop hoped their hiding place was a secret, but in espionage, one could never be sure. Li seemed relieved to leave the mounting tension in the room behind.

Sitting himself at the table, Bishop realised he was famished. Although he normally treated his body like a temple, consuming only the cleanest and most nutrient-rich plant-based food, Bishop tore open a packet of panda cookies and poured it into his mouth. Before he'd properly finished chewing, he filled Tessa and Argento in on his activities since leaving them at the police station, right up to the part about Chang's demise courtesy of a trip through the windscreen. He conveniently left out one piece of information. When he was finished, he leaned back, even more exhausted.

"You're wrong about one thing there, son." Argento's demeanour was as gruff as when Bishop had first entered the room. "Chang's not dead."

Bishop scoffed. "I saw him exiting a van in a method not at all recommended by the manufacturer."

Argento frowned. "Be that as it may, The Pope messaged me. The son of a bitch is in hospital. Cuts and abrasions, but he's expected to make a full recovery. That's one lucky evil bastard."

Bishop took on this new information and reviewed his

strategy. It still held. In fact, some pieces fit far better. Before he could move forward, he needed information. And its purveyor was right in front of him.

Bishop glared at Argento. "What's your favourite album, Kevin?"

Argento rolled his eyes. "Jimmy No-Teeth sings Burt Bacharach in Yiddish."

With a frown, Bishop nodded. "And your favourite colour?"

"Whatever your eyes are. Is bloodshot a colour?" Argento sighed. "Can we get on with it now that you've baselined me?"

"Baselined?" Tessa was leaning forward, frowning, attempting to keep up.

With a shrug, Bishop explained, "Set up questions you know the answer to, or that they have no reason to lie in response to, then you have a baseline going forward."

With a sneer, Argento studied his fingernails. "Unless, of course, your subject taught his ungrateful little shit interrogator the technique—then the point is somewhat moot." He turned to Bishop. "I'm fine, by the way, thank you for asking. Your concern for my wellbeing gives me the warm tinglies."

Bishop ignored the bait. He had to keep it professional. "Kevin, what the fuck is going on?"

Semi-professional.

The old man waggled a green packet at Bishop. "I'm trying to figure out if these are chicken flavoured or not."

Bishop was all business. "That's not what I was asking."

"I know what you meant, son." Argento was snappy. He knew the moment was long overdue. "You mean why the hell have I been shooting up half of China and starting World War Three?"

"Pretty much."

Argento leaned forward. "I'm actually trying to stop World War Three."

"I'll be the judge of that, if you don't mind." Leaning back, Bishop folded his arms. "Make it good."

And he did. Within five minutes, Argento had laid out his story.

Three months ago, he was doing exactly what Tessa and Bishop thought he was doing: being a leisurely retiree and keeping to himself. Well, for the most part. When he wasn't wandering the local township and doing odd jobs around the house, he quietly kept an eye on China. Not all of it, just certain people.

"Like who?" Bishop asked.

"Certain people." Argento's tone was firm, clearly telling Bishop not to ask any more.

Bishop asked more. "Would these Chinese happen to be naval related? Asking for a friend."

Argento sighed. "Yes. Fine. Those bastards who killed my son. Our government could coddle the great Chinese government all they liked, but there was no way in hell a multi-billion-dollar vessel had a GPS glitch and strayed into Chinese territorial waters. That's as likely as me shaving my legs and dancing at the Moulin Rouge."

"I've seen you dance, Dad. No one wants that."

Tessa's attempt at humour did nothing to lighten the mood. Both men were all business. Argento went on.

One day he dug deeper and found that each of the men Argento held responsible for his son's death had received promotions in quick succession. When Bishop challenged it, Argento conceded it wasn't unusual for military personnel to receive advancement following a military engagement. It was the *nature* of the promotions that caught Argento's attention. Some were ordinary promotions, many others were due to the incumbent meeting mysterious and seemingly convenient ends. The signature on almost all of these was Chang's.

"Wait, wait." Bishop held up his hand. "Where did you get this information? It's not like the Chinese military detail their staff movements in a weekly newsletter."

For the first time since Bishop had known him, Argento seemed sheepish. He frowned, then gave a shrug.

Bishop shook his head. "The Pope fed you all this, didn't he?"

"Not all of it... enough."

In retrospect, Bishop shouldn't have been surprised. He motioned for Argento to continue.

Soon The Pope had flags on all the key players and the alerts came thick and fast. Each moved up the ranks like wildfire. In his words, something was fishier than a halibut milkshake.

Argento made a call to an Assistant Secretary of GCHQ, Carol Gray. She'd previously worked at MI6 and was the one who had lured him from SAS in the first place. Her final act at MI6 before she left had been to sponsor Argento's replication of the endeavour, which had eventually lured Bishop into MI6. Without her, Bishop mused, he wouldn't be sitting where he was at that moment in time.

Out of respect for their friendship Gray agreed to meet, but Argento could tell she didn't think there was much in it. They arranged a get-together halfway between London and Keswick. They met in a tiny tea room and she told Argento she didn't have long. In fact, Argento recalled, she didn't even take off her coat. He wasted no time laying out his evidence and showing how far the power play went.

Ever the devil's advocate, Carol questioned many of Argento's assertions. She had a point. A person building an empire wasn't uncommon, even on that scale. Both MI6 and GCHQ had gone through spates of individuals attempting to shore up their power base by building a mini-empire. Why was this any different?

Then Argento dropped his trump card. Chang.

The golden child of the Chinese navy, the poster boy for all aspirational naval cadets and the hero of the encounter with the English suddenly up and quit. Not only that, he made the unprecedented move from naval admiral to the head of the Ministry of State Security. Gray took off her coat and ordered another pot of tea.

"I assumed he was busted out of the navy." Bishop shrugged. "That they did it to placate the West after such a major international incident."

"Since when do the Chinese do anything to placate anyone?" Argento opened another can of Pepsi. "Chang was offered a promotion within the navy and treated as a hero. The hard-as-nails leader who gave the West a bloody nose. He could write his own ticket. Then, boom, he left the navy and went straight into the Ministry of State Security. That makes zero sense, right? A high-flying, respected and blooded naval admiral suddenly becoming the head of their security service? That's like an astronaut suddenly becoming the Head of Neuroscience. Something didn't add up."

To Bishop, the information Argento had laid out was worthy of opening a case file and investigating further, but hardly justified taking on China single-handedly. There had to be more. He hoped there was more.

There was. Carol left more rattled than she'd arrived. Over the next two weeks she launched her own investigation, off the books. It turned up far more than The Pope and Argento had managed in months of investigation. It quickly became evident that what they'd uncovered was less a grasp for power and more like a revolution. Key members of cabinet suddenly retired or met with sudden and violent ends. More of Chang's people turned up in key positions. The move that had both Gray and Argento most worried was when one of his lieutenants was appointed to the National People's Congress and within weeks joined the Defence committee.

"The same one you shot up in that farm?" Bishop recalled the incident that had sent him on the mission.

Argento nodded. "It was obvious there was a power play going down, but no one but Carol and I seemed aware of it."

"Can Carol confirm this?"

"Probably not." Argento took a swig from his Pepsi. "She's dead." He let it float in the air a few seconds. "Died a day after she called me about the defence ministry appointment. It was a home invasion gone wrong, they said. Some punk broke into her house to steal the keys to her Range Rover, they said. My wrinkly arse it was. That woman was as tough as twenty-year-old beef jerky. No way anyone searching for a cheap thrill would have stood a chance against her. She could freeze your blood with a stare—and this is coming from an ex-SAS paratrooper. They invented the word formidable just for her. No, the woman was murdered, plain and simple."

Bishop let that sink in. One or two of the things Argento had laid out could be viewed in different ways, but not all. There were too many.

Now he understood why Argento had gone rogue. If the GCHQ, the intelligence organisation for signals intelligence, had moles, nowhere was safe. No one could be trusted.

"It wasn't a farm he was visiting, was it? The one you tried to assassinate, Chang's man?"

Argento smiled for the first time, relieved that Bishop

finally got it. "No. The farm was just a front, it was newly laid foundation for an underground nuclear missile silo."

"Newly installed? That's a major provocative move. China's a signatory on the Non-Proliferation Treaty. They shouldn't be building new silos unless…"

"Exactly." Argento nodded. "Chang's people are not only building an empire, they're assembling an arsenal for war. With key members in the army, navy, intelligence community, defence committee and within the party itself, Chang is setting himself up as dictator."

Bishop nodded. "So you took it upon yourself to take him down single-handedly?"

"I have the skills—at least I used to. There would be plausible deniability, as no one sent me. Plus, there was the small fact that anyone who knew about the situation ended up dead. It was something I had to do alone."

Having remained silent during the exchange, Tessa placed her hand over her father's. "You were never alone, Dad."

"I know, Poppet." His grin was remorseful. "I was doing this for you. I didn't want any grandkid of mine growing up in the shadow of nuclear war like I did." He patted his daughter's hand. "I knew I couldn't get to Chang, at least not initially. So… I decided to get his attention by taking out his people, one by one. Seemed to work."

"You don't say?" Bishop couldn't help admiring the old coot. Despite being well past his prime, he had achieved so much and remained alive long enough to tell the tale. Argento seemed prouder of his achievements now that he knew Bishop understood his actions.

"How do you know you were right about the silos?" Bishop asked. "I understand that members of defence committees probably don't usually visit farms, but are you sure they were actually silos? Did you see them?"

Argento frowned, as if conceding the point, but Bishop knew he was doing nothing of the sort. "I would agree with you except for a few minor things. One, farms don't usually have excavations running a hundred feet down, nor do they have blueprints with awfully missile-shaped diagrams. Rice paddies normally have, you know, rice. But I might just be a senile old man." Even Argento had to smile at his own sarcasm. "And as for the final reason, well, at the risk of sounding far too mysterious, I'll tell you later."

"Now's not a good time?" Bishop folded his arms.

"A girl can't give everything up on the first date. You'll have to wine and dine me first." Argento gave Bishop a wide grin. He had something, something good, but wasn't willing to give it up just yet. He'd wait until it was strategically advantageous. Once a spy…

Argento leaned over and squeezed his former pupil's shoulder. "You understand now, don't you?"

Bishop nodded. Argento was insanely brave to have taken this on single-handedly. Bishop knew he probably would have done the same thing.

"Taking out the *Albion* was their first ham-fisted try. Chang's people facilitated the launch of a GPS satellite to make the *Albion* think it was somewhere else entirely. The Chinese could then claim, quite accurately, that they had fired upon a vessel invading their territorial waters."

"You have proof?"

"I have confessions."

Bishop frowned. "Not quite the same thing." He scratched the back of his neck. "What does Chang want out of all this?"

"A better question is what does he want China to have after all this? He's a patriot—an insane one, but a patriot nonetheless. A fanatic. What does he want? Oh, not much. Taiwan. The actual Taiwan, not just in name.

Matsu Islands and Arunachal Pradesh… any disputed territories, really. A stranglehold on Hong Kong—the 'one country, two systems' isn't really working to their advantage as they'd hoped. Probably a few more territories too, if this really goes to hell. Chang's thinking is that China is the economic powerhouse of the twenty-first century, so it's about time they flexed some military and political muscle."

"But that's…"

"What the US did one hundred years before? Exactly. America broke from years of isolationism to become a global juggernaut. What Chang's doing will be written in the history books a thousand years from now."

"They're going to have books a thousand years from now?" Tessa's words may have been humorous, but her tone was far from it.

Argento gave his daughter a sympathetic smile and turned to Bishop. "A few years ago China announced that their army was no longer just for defence. There are some in their government who want to show it, led by Chang."

Bishop had to concede that what Argento was saying was plausible. "Assuming all this is true, what did you expect to achieve by killing everyone?"

"Not everyone, just those responsible."

"Responsible for Ashley's death?"

"Some. But most came in after that. Chang won acolytes by showing them he had the ability to back up his insane plans. Goad the West and win without them even knowing? He'd already done it. What I've been doing isn't about revenge, Charles. This is about preventing more deaths. More Ashleys. I'm doing what my government never would."

With steepled fingers, Bishop said, "If I were to play devil's advocate—"

"Oh, that would be a change." Argento crossed his arms.

Bishop ignored him. "Chang's lust for power could be viewed as a purely internal matter. The *Albion* aside, Chang's moves are about getting him into power."

"Oh god, son, haven't you been listening? What the hell did I teach you? China's not going to start a war, they'll finish it. Chang's aim is to incite the West into aggressive action. China knows it can't just go and claim Matsu Islands or Arunachal Pradesh. But if they're attacked, and they fight back and win, who's to stop them claiming a few extra territories here and there? To the victor goes the spoils, right? Millions will die in a war manufactured by Chang. That's what this is all about: China claiming its rightful place in history."

"What you've given me is all fine and good, worth checking out, but nothing shows Chang as a *specific* international threat, someone who—"

"Project Dragon Sun."

Bishop shook his head. "I'm sorry, what?"

Argento's features carried an element of smugness. He'd been waiting for this moment. "Project Dragon Sun. That's Chang's little scheme. A bug has been placed in the US Navy's tracking software. During next month's Han Kuang joint military exercise, including the US and Taiwan, the bug will launch an attack at an incoming YJ-18 anti-ship missile, which will actually turn out to be a Chinese civilian airliner. The flight will also contain several members of the party who Chang wishes to remove. I'm surprised it doesn't come with a nice pretty bow."

"How—" Bishop started.

"A little chat I had with Yao Qing, who was, officially, a cultural attaché to the UN. He took some coaxing, but was rather forthcoming in the end."

"And you slit his throat for it." Bishop kept his voice even, not wanting to stop him talking.

He dared not look at Tessa. She must have suspected what her father was capable of, but having it confirmed was another matter entirely.

Argento shrugged. "Then there's Project Buddha's Fist. This one took some balls to even conceive, let me tell you. Zhou Cai told me, after bawling like a baby and begging for his life. Honestly, I expected more of a Commander of the Ministry of State Security." He frowned. "Buddha's Fist is breathtaking. Forged intelligence will show that China is massing forces along the McMahon Line, preparing an all-out offensive to shore up the disputed Arunachal Pradesh. The US will be goaded into launching a pre-emptive attack. Just as they do, it will be revealed that the intelligence was forged in order for the US to assign ownership to India once and for all. In exchange, the US was to get a sweet free-trade deal in the world's largest expanding market. Of course, China will fight back, crush opposition and finally take the land they've been manoeuvring for since the Sino-Indian war. And as far as the rest of the world is concerned, China was just defending herself. You can't blame a victim from striking back, now can you? Chang's quite mad, but the frightening thing is, he's winning. His people are almost all in place, his power grows by the hour. There are more of these plans, if you'd like me to go on."

"No, that won't be necessary." Bishop's mind whirled. "What's our armament situation?"

Argento gave him a curious expression. "Better than most nation states. We raided another of Chang's stashes before we arrived. We could effectively invade Iceland, or Greenland, even the Falklands. Any of the lands, really."

"England?"

"Okay, not all, but we could probably take Wales by tea time. Chang was primarily arming for a conflict."

Bishop frowned thoughtfully. "Then that's what we'll give him."

Argento furrowed his brow. "And why would we do that?"

"To end this."

Li walked into the room and took a chocolate bar from the pile on the table. "End what?"

Bishop's mind was whirring. "Everything."

Argento gave Bishop a wry grin and leaned back with his hands behind his head. It was an expression Bishop remembered well. "I would have thought you'd be calling for extraction at the first opportunity."

"Normally, yes." Bishop placed his own hands behind his head, mirroring his old mentor. "But what if we don't?"

"Don't what?"

"Don't call for an extraction team." Bishop smiled. "I mean, we could, obviously. Then MI6 would know about Chang's plans, sure, but we can cover that off in a report that I can send in twenty minutes. If we leave China, Chang will still be in a position of power. He'll still be able to carry out his plans. What use is knowledge if you can't do anything about it?"

"We'd be like Cassandra." Li's face lit up; he was finally able to contribute to the conversation.

"Yes, exactly." Bishop's face darkened. "No, wait, who?"

"Cassandra. From mythology. She could see into the future, but no one believed her."

"But," Tessa rubbed her chin, "that's not exactly the case here. MI6 will believe us, they just won't be able to do anything about it. There are parallels, sure, but—"

"Is this a mission briefing or a history debate?"

Argento's annoyance was as plain as the veins on the sides of his temples. "Chang has dozens of murderous trained killers out there. I would have thought the most pressing topic would be getting my daughter to safety, not an ancient Roman—"

"It's Greek." Li pursed his lips in regret.

With teeth as clenched as his fists, Argento inhaled. "Be that as it may, we have more pressing matters."

"Yes, we do," Bishop interjected. "Like finishing this. Finishing Chang."

Argento frowned. "A noble sentiment, but in order to end this you're going to need some sort of magic trick up your sleeve. Do you have one of those?"

"Actually, yes, I do." Bishop found an apple hidden beneath all the junk food. He took a bite and grinned. "She's downstairs in the van and probably really hungry by now."

CHAPTER TWELVE

The three of them stared, dumbstruck, as Bishop led Zhao into the conference room. Back at the crash site he'd wanted her dead. He could easily have wrung the life from her unconscious body, but the moment passed quickly. At the time he'd thought Chang was gone, meaning Zhao was the only one who could tell them what had truly been going on. Her purpose had changed, but the end goal remained the same.

Bound with plumber's tape, blindfolded and barefoot, she more closely resembled a mummy than a double agent. Bishop removed the blindfold and pushed Zhao towards a seat in the corner of the room, far away from any exit.

"Sit in the corner. If you behave we might let you lick the inside of a crisp packet."

Across the room, Tessa said nothing, viewing the new arrival with curiosity. Her eyes darted between Zhao and Bishop, as if trying to determine how they felt about each other.

"He's going to kill you for this." Zhao's words were dipped in poison. "If you thought he was formidable before, you have no idea what he'll be like when he finds out you've taken me."

"Oh, you mean Chang? Yeah, I don't think that's going to be an issue." Bishop's tone was genial. "You see, he's dead."

Zhao gulped.

"Don't you remember him hurtling through that windscreen? Like a frozen chicken… uh, through a windscreen. Sorry, that didn't work, did it? I'm sure I had something for this. Hang on…"

He glanced up as if contemplating the perfect quip. He wasn't. He was giving Zhao time to process what he'd said. Bishop had found that lies were always more believable when laced with the truth. If Zhao recalled Chang careening through the windscreen, his supposed death would seem much more plausible. And with her mentor apparently dead, she wouldn't be worried about betraying him later, when the interrogation began.

At least, that was the theory.

Fighting back tears, Zhao's face slowly morphed into unbridled anger. "*You* killed him! You killed the man who made me, who lifted me from nothing! *You're* nothing. You're not worthy to lick his boots. You have no idea what you've done."

"Oh, I think I do, Zhao." Bishop tilted his head. "Do you don't mind if I still call you Zhao? I assume you have a real name, but Zhao saves confusion." Without waiting for a response, he went on. "What I've done, Zhao, is stopped a crazy powerplay, unprecedented in China's modern era—oh yes, and prevented a world war." Bishop slammed his fists on the table, making Tessa and Li jump. Argento didn't flinch. "I've stopped a madman hellbent on destabilising China and the world. So, I know perfectly well what I've done!" His anger was only half genuine, but it held her attention.

The irony of Bishop boasting about having achieved something that was yet to happen—Chang's demise—was not lost on him. If he failed to retrieve the information from Zhao, Chang's death would not come to pass. He could indeed succeed, shift the balance of nuclear power and trigger a war. It all came down to the next hour.

"Now…" Bishop walked around the table and leaned over Zhao. "… I have one important question, and for the love of god, you'd better answer truthfully." Face as hard as concrete, he leaned closer. "Tomato or chicken?"

"What… what?"

"Crisps." Bishop went to the table and picked up two packets of Lay's. "I've tried the French Chicken flavour and it honestly tastes like Paris."

Zhao failed to mask the confusion on her face, but hunger won out. She nodded towards the "Little Tomato" flavoured packet. Bishop's key interrogation strategy was to keep the prey off kilter. He fed her a handful of chips, followed by some water. She seemed calmer; either she realised that her outburst had achieved nothing, or she was sated by the food.

Zhao poked her chin towards him. "What do you want from me?"

"You, Zhao, are the Rosetta stone codebook lynchpin."

"Mixed metaphor much?" Tessa raised an eyebrow.

"Shhh. Don't interrupt me when I'm being smug."

"If we didn't, no one would get a word in." Tessa was clearly amused at her comeback.

Bishop couldn't argue, so he ignored Tessa and addressed Zhao. "You're going to colour in the last few patches of the picture I'll stick on the fridge at MI6. And if you stay within the lines and fill in all the right colours, you might even live. How does that sound?"

Zhao spat in his face.

Wiping the saliva away, Bishop smirked. "Mmm, tomato-flavoured spit, my favourite." He straightened his back. "If that's the way you're going to play it, I'll be back in a minute."

Bishop strode out of the conference room and Tessa followed quickly behind. Realising he'd been left behind with Argento and Zhao, Li launched himself out of the room behind the other two. Argento reluctantly followed.

All four stood out of earshot in the offensively plain hallway.

Tessa cocked an eyebrow. "She's pretty."

"Is she?" Bishop did his best to remain neutral.

"Don't be daft. Of course she's pretty. She's pretty, isn't she Li?"

"Ah, look." Li scratched the back of his head. "To be honest, girls aren't really my thing."

"I kind of guessed." Tessa gave him a warm smile. "But you can appreciate her appearance in an academic sense, right?"

"I guess so. Yeah, she's pretty."

"See?" She turned to her father. "You would have thought her pretty when you saw her, wouldn't you, Dad?"

Argento scowled. "To be honest, the first time I saw her she was naked, so I'm staying out of this conversation completely, if that's quite alright."

Having made her point, Tessa turned to Bishop. "You left her in the van all this time?" She planted her fists on her hips. "Why the hell did you wait for Dad to tell you everything before you brought her out?"

"You pretty much just answered your own question. I didn't know your father's story, or why he was doing what he was. He could have been a madman; he could have done anything when I brought her out. Shot her, kidnapped her and run off, used her head as a hat, I had no idea."

Argento crossed his arms. "Charming."

"And now that you know Dad's not the madman?"

"I'm standing right here, Poppet."

Bishop's face was suddenly devoid of all humour. "Now we get some answers."

He sent everyone back into the conference room and told them not to engage the prisoner. It only took a few minutes to retrieve the tool he needed from the plumber's van. He had no idea of the level of Zhao's resistance to interrogation training. He had to suppose it was formidable. He'd have to cut through it. Literally.

Storming through the boardroom door, he strode straight over to Zhao with a set of bolt cutters in hand.

Fear smacked across Zhao's face. "What... what are you..." She cowered, her bound arms clawing at the wall.

"I don't have fucking time."

Bishop seized Zhao's foot and placed her left little toe of between the blades. In one smooth movement, he sliced it clean off. Her agonised scream came from the very depths of her soul. Everyone in the room reeled in shock.

Waving the bloody blades in her face, Bishop shouted over her shrieks. "And we're only just getting started. There are two hundred and five more bones in your human body. Now give me answers!"

The interrogation went on for another hour, not as brutal as its commencement, but ruthlessly efficient. Bishop was relentless, using every technique he'd ever learned.

Tessa stood in the corner of the room, stunned. Despite frequent requests from Bishop for her to leave, she resolutely stayed. It was the first time she'd ever seen Bishop, the professional. The blunt instrument.

Bishop wondered if she understood that this side of him, the efficient weapon side, was all thanks to her father's tutelage. Argento had turned Bishop from an efficient soldier into a lethal spy.

The stunned expression on her face suggested she'd never imagined him capable of such ruthlessness. Whatever flickering hope of reconciliation he'd nurtured was finally extinguished. She'd finally seen who he really was.

All the hard-heartedness worked, though. Bishop's relentless interrogation had broken through. They had the information.

One of the first pieces was Zhao's real name: Liu Yandong. That was phase one in breaking her down. The rest flowed far easier. Her words soon became a flood. Her history with Chang was the first topic.

Chang had spotted her early in her career, a bright graduate who breezed through basic training. As a senior member of the Navy, Chang took her under his wing and nurtured her ascension through the ranks. She was the prodigy, he the mentor.

Bishop had been right to spare her life. She held the key to everything. Through tears of pain and anger, she continued to talk, whether from fear, grief, or simply because she needed to.

Just as Bishop had with Argento, she'd followed Chang into the Ministry of State Security. That's when the topic of the interrogation changed. As they'd suspected, Chang's ultimate objective stretched far beyond the Ministry. Beyond even his own country's political ambitions. The framework that Chang was establishing would reverberate around the world for decades. The plans were apparently magnificent in their audacity.

"What does he want? What is Chang after?"

Zhao frowned. She was pale, wearied, but still had her wits about her. Her eyes narrowed. "Nothing. He was doing nothing but pushing forward the inevitable."

Bishop offered no reply, letting the silence urge Zhao forward.

She went on. "My entire life, from my first years of schooling, like everyone else in my country, I was told that this century was China's century. Ours. The dominance of the European powers was finally at an end. Your in-fighting started the cancer, and you never recovered. The European Union is nothing but death by bureaucracy. For a brief shining moment, the United States had their time, but they, too, sabotaged themselves, and their fall will be long and painful. Now is China's time once more. We have always been the leader in so many things but now, this century, we will dominate the world. Your old structures, your old systems are holding us back. Your old empires, desperately clinging to their outmoded spheres of influence, will no longer hold sway over us. Chang would have changed it all. He would have brought forward what will happen eventually; his brilliance would have made it manifest before its time." She lowered her face. "Until you murdered him."

"I'm… I'm gobsmacked." Bishop shook his head in awe.

Zhao nodded. "He was an amazing man."

"No." Bishop shook his head. "I'm gobsmacked that you spoke so long without actually saying anything. If I had a pound for every time I've come across a self-fellating delusional megalomaniac, I'd have approximately twelve pounds fifty." He pulled up a seat and picked up the bolt cutters. "What," he watched the bloody blades open and close several times, "was Chang *actually* doing? Any more vagaries about making China great again will result in more little piggies going to market."

Staring at him with a mixture of hatred and fear, Zhao's expression finally fell. It was the look of someone resigned to their fate. She had no fight left.

"Why did Chang want to start a war?"

Zhao gave a crooked grin. "He would never start the war. He'd finish it."

They were similar to the words Argento had spoken. Bishop's old mentor gently placed his hand on Bishop's shoulder and nodded towards Zhao, as if asking, *may I have a turn?* No longer the hunched, exhausted retiree, he had the stance of the man Bishop remembered, his old mentor in his prime. There was fire in his belly once again.

Bishop glanced at Argento and opened his palm towards Zhao. *Be my guest.*

Argento paced. "You're Chang's acolyte, yes? The one he calls Little Dove? I tried finding you, but it seems you found me first."

Zhao's lips were white and cracked. "I don't know what you're talking about."

Argento nodded, as if expecting the response. Bishop knew him well enough to know he was playing with her. Circling for the kill.

"As his Little Dove, you'd be privy to all your mentor's plans, his key advisors, contact protocols and the like."

"I know nothing of—"

"It's okay, you're not betraying him if he's dead, are you?" Without waiting for a reply, he went on. "What about Project Dragon Sun?"

Zhao's eyes went wide.

"Project Buddha's Fist? Heavenly Realm? Tiger Claw?"

"I… I… How do you know…"

"Oh, Little Dove, you're not cut out for espionage if you're going to drop your guard so easily."

Zhao did her best to recover her composure, but it was a futile effort. The war had been fought and lost. She had all but confirmed the existence of the plans.

"Bishop, be a dear, would you?" Argento's words were pleasant, his tone anything but. "Grab the bolt cutters. Every time Little Dove here lies about the plans, remove another one of her toes. By the time we get to her fingers we should be getting somewhere."

Bishop stood and grabbed the implement. Both Zhao and Tessa gasped. Not sure if Argento was bluffing or not, Bishop walked straight over to Zhao and slapped her bound hands away to put the pinkie toe of her right foot between the blades. He turned to Argento and nodded, as if to say, *when you're ready.*

"Please, no, please!" Zhao's voice broke, and tears ran down her face. "Dragon Sun's to intercept war games and down an airliner; Buddha's Fist's is to take back Arunachal Pradesh, Heavenly Realm, Matsu Islands. Taiwan is under Tiger Claw. Please stop!"

Argento picked up a packet of crisps and crunched on one. Bishop knew it was all show. He was performing, Zhao his lone audience member. Turning to Bishop, he raised an eyebrow. There may as well have been a giant neon sign above his head saying, *told you so.* The two old colleagues shared a smirk.

Bishop stepped back and put the bolt cutters down. They wouldn't need them again.

"How big is Chang's cadre? How many men could he call on?"

Zhao's eyes darted between the bolt cutters on the floor and her bandaged foot, lingering on the red stain where her toe used to be. Her shoulders sagged. "No more than two hundred, but they're well placed. They had access to all they needed to rewrite the world. And you killed him. You're a monster."

Bishop shrugged indifferently. "Chang had a deadline, he admitted as much back in the van. What did he need before Friday?"

Zhao turned to Argento. "Ask him. It was all his fault."

Bishop did just that. "Care to fill in the blanks, Kevin?"

"Remember that piece of information I was withholding about the brand-new missile silos?"

There was a tiny whimper from Zhao. They knew all her dirty little secrets.

Argento smiled. "The last time the Chinese built a missile silo was in the early seventies. They've been sporadically maintained since then. The thing is, they're so old they're well and truly mapped. Hell, you spend five minutes googling, you can find them yourself. Chang's people laid the foundations of a new set, meaning they'd have a significant bargaining chip when they eventually sat down at the negotiation table. They'd know where all the US missiles are but not the other way around. Quite the advantage, no?"

Bishop could see Argento was heading somewhere, but he wasn't sure where. He shrugged, as if to say, *and?*

"I took this off one of the goons when I was at the farm-slash-missile silo." Argento hefted a yellow plastic briefcase with sticker on the side—a triangle, with a yellow and black circle design. "You don't usually bring one of these when you visit a farm."

"Is that—"

"The nuclear launch protocols for the new set of ICBMs the Chinese have been developing on the side."

He let that sink in for a moment.

Nodding towards the case, Bishop frowned. "Is it still active?"

Argento shrugged. "Probably."

"Wouldn't they change the codes?"

"To do that, Chang would have had to admit he'd given it to his man, who'd lost it. Not a good look for someone who doesn't have all his people in place yet."

Bishop finally understood. "That's what Chang was after. It wasn't you. He wanted the damn case. He had to get it back before its absence was discovered on Friday." He turned to Zhao, who nodded. "All he cared about when he tortured me was that bloody case."

"Sorry about that, but yes." Argento rubbed his whiskers. "It seems I finally got his attention."

"Wow." Tessa sighed. "That's why those guys tried to kidnap me on the street after I left Bishop's apartment. They wanted to use me to get to you, so you'd hand over the case."

Argento swivelled to his daughter. "You were at his apartment?"

"Dad, not exactly the key takeaway from that sentence."

"First things first," Bishop interrupted, happy to change the subject. "We have something Chang wants. We have an opportunity to end this."

"Something Chang wants..." Horror crossed Zhao's face. "You said he was dead!"

Holding his hands up with a *what are you gonna do* expression, Bishop leaned towards Zhao. "And you said you were an MI6 agent. Don't take the moral high horse with me. Your horse is very low. Like a Shetland pony."

Anger morphed into confusion. "What are you on about?"

"I actually don't know anymore. It's been a long day."

"But he's alive? Chang's alive?" Hope radiated from

Zhao, but her face soon hardened. She muttered in Chinese.

Li's head jerked around. "Damn, girl!"

Zhao lowered her head and kept murmuring with intent, her eyes transfixed on Bishop.

"What's she saying?"

"It's… it's not nice, dude. I mean… shit, girl! You kiss your mother with that… oh, that's fucking nasty!" Li covered his mouth with his hand. "You can't say—now look, I'm almost certain that's physically impossible."

Zhao kept cursing. Bishop ignored her. It was time for a change in tactic. It was time for action.

Chang was a power-hungry tyrant, willing to sacrifice millions for his own ends. And they had something he wanted. More than one thing.

Argento turned to Bishop. The younger man sensed that his old mentor was reading his mind. "You're the ranking officer on this mission. What happens now?"

Bishop smiled. "That's up to Zhao."

She stopped her guttural cursing and glared at Bishop, surprised. "Me? Why me?"

Bishop picked up a phone and held it in front of her tear-stained face. "Be a chum and give old Chang a call, would you? Tell him to come rescue you. Oh, and you might want to mention that we still have the case. Tell him he has two hours or his Little Dove will lose more than her toe. Be convincing. I know you're good at that."

Li looked on in horror. "What are you going to do, man?"

Bishop's eyes shone. "End this."

CHAPTER THIRTEEN

All around the city was desolate rubble. No tree grew, no hill interrupted the horizon; the landscape was as flat as the bottom of an anvil. It had been an hour and a half since Zhao had called Chang. The conversation had been brief and to the point. They were waiting for Chang in Long Cheng. In return for Zhao and the case, they wanted a fast car and no tail. Everyone knew that would never happen. During the brief phone call, Zhao's eyes had repeatedly darted between the bolt cutters and Bishop. It was all over in less than two minutes.

Now they waited.

From atop an apartment block—the tallest point in the city—Bishop scanned the landscape on all sides. He had no doubt Chang would come. With such valuable ransom, an airstrike was unlikely. But he would come.

The door to the stairwell creaked behind him. Bishop didn't turn. He knew who it was. It was long overdue.

"I never hated you, you know?"

Bishop turned to see Argento standing with a bottle of Chivas Regal in hand. "I know."

Argento sat next to Bishop and took a drink. "It's… it's just, she's my little girl, and I knew what you were capable of, what you'd done professionally. She deserved…"

"Better."

"No, that's not what I was going to say." Argento offered the bottle to Bishop. "She'll never do better than you, son. No, I was going to say happy. She deserved to be happy. Oh, you would have tried, but with what you do, what you're good at, you'd only bring pain. You'd never have made my Tessa happy."

Bishop took a swig of Chivas. "I would have, you know."

Argento frowned, amused. "Did you leave the service?"

"You know I didn't."

"Because you can't." Argento took the bottle back. "And that's why you'd never make her happy."

"Always with the lessons."

"I'll stop as soon as you stop needing them."

The warm air swirled around them. Argento took a drink.

"I never got to say how sorry I was about Ashley."

"I knew, son. Believe me, I knew."

They were silent for a time. A lot remained unsaid, but far more was understood.

"I've missed you, you old coot."

"I've missed you, you young idiot."

They shared a genuine smile for the first time in years, and the time fell away like old skin. Bishop had his mentor back; the teacher had his pupil. Argento's hand slapped down on the young man's shoulder and he sucked in air. He swallowed hard, his eyes glassy. An unspoken covenant had been reached, and they were friends once more. Just like that.

"Nice day." The old man cast his eyes skyward. "Think it'll be our last?"

"Not if everyone carried out my orders."

"What if that's not enough?"

Bishop gazed up. "Then at least it's a nice day."

Argento nodded. He took a swig from the bottle, left it beside Bishop and stood. His bones creaked.

"Bishop?"

"Hmmm?"

"You look after my Tessa. There's not a man alive I trust more than you to do that. You do whatever it takes to keep her safe."

"You know I will."

"I do. But I had to say it all the same."

Turning, Argento walked back to the stairwell. As he reached the door, he glanced over his shoulder. "And Charles… You left Nathan Vincent behind a long time ago." A sad expression crossed his face. "I don't think I've ever said it, but I'm honoured you've lived up to the name I gave you."

Not waiting for a reply, Argento disappeared into the stairwell. Bishop stared at the void where he'd stood. Unable to stop it, a sob escaped the younger man.

Like many men of his generation, Argento had never been big on sharing his emotions. What he'd said would have been hard. And Bishop knew it came from the heart.

Surveying the barren surrounds of the abandoned city, Bishop became lost in thought, memories and emotions tumbling over one another. It was all too much. He controlled his breathing, tried to focus, and abruptly caught himself in a microsleep. He was running on fumes. He'd been moving virtually nonstop since landing in China.

The next few hours would determine if all their efforts amounted to anything. But the words of his old mentor resonated. *Keep Tessa safe.* Not because she was a feeble woman—far from it. Because you protected the ones you loved.

Behind him, Bishop heard quiet footfalls. "I was just thinking about you."

Tessa sat beside him, cross-legged. "Should I be concerned?"

"Oh, don't worry," Bishop handed her the Chivas, "it was completely inappropriate."

"Phew." She took a swig. "You had me worried there for a second."

"Speaking of, remember the Ambassador's cloakroom and how they asked us to leave?"

Tessa choked on the Chivas, amused. "If I recall correctly, they told us to put our clothes on and said if we ever came back they'd have us up on indecency charges."

"Fun times." Bishop took the bottle back and drank.

"We were different people back then."

"I'm glad you didn't say innocent."

Tessa smiled. "No, we definitely weren't that." She sighed and stroked his cheek. "But we've changed since then. You certainly have."

"You say that with intent. Something on your mind?" Bishop offered her the bottle again.

She shook her head. "I shouldn't. Need to stay focused."

Bishop waited for her to go on, but received only silence. "You were going to say something."

Tessa nodded. "I always tried to block it out, what you were doing when you were away. But it always snuck in. Especially when you came back with bruises and cuts, and always a distant expression, like a part of you was still back wherever you'd just been. Over time, less and less of you came back." She inhaled deeply and looked to the sky. They were quiet for a moment.

"She's pretty."

It was Bishop's turn to smile. "Zhao? Is that jealousy I hear?"

A shrug. "No, just an observation."

"Sometimes it's difficult to tell the difference."

"And sometimes it isn't." Tessa gestured towards the stairs. "You didn't baseline her."

"I'm sorry?"

"Zhao. You didn't baseline her like you did with Dad."

"There really was no need. I'd already seen her lie. Extremely convincingly. It's when her mouth moves."

Tessa nodded. "So how can we believe anything she said during the interrogation?"

"We can't."

Her face fell. "But... but your whole plan is based on what she said."

"Exactly. Welcome to espionage. Fun, isn't it?"

"Fun isn't the word I'd choose, Charles."

He shrugged and scanned the empty horizon. "Your dad said something that got me thinking."

"Oh, this can't be good."

"Would we have worked out, Tessa? If it wasn't for '6, I mean?"

"Maybe. I don't know. Relationships are hard."

"I know."

"Do you? There's more to a relationship than deciding who sleeps in the wet patch, you know." Her words weren't harsh, just weary.

Bishop nudged her. "I have a feeling you swerved the conversation somewhat. What did you really want to say, Tessa? Back before you skilfully sidestepped talking about Zhao."

She grinned a paper-thin grin and shrugged, as if to say, *you got me.* "The way you interrogated her ... even when you knew I was there… I never imagined… it's like I knew you and didn't know you at the same time."

"I'm doing my job, Tessa."

"I know. Believe me, I know. But it's one thing to suspect something; it's completely another to have it confirmed. There was a ruthlessness to what you did." She held up a hand to halt his protest. "I'm not saying you took pleasure in it. But you're the man I always feared you could be. A man I don't know."

"A man you don't want to know?"

The wind washed over them. The air seemed chillier. A flock of birds took flight in the distance.

Tessa watched the birds. "We should get in position."

Placing his hand gently on her arm, Bishop said, "I asked you a question, Tessa."

She turned to face him. "I know. I can't answer it. Not because I don't want to, but because I don't know. I honestly don't know."

Bishop nodded. "That's fair. I appreciate your honesty."

She stood and rubbed his shoulder. "Honesty was never our problem."

As she walked away, a million thoughts swirled in his mind. He tried to stamp them down. There were other things he needed to concentrate on.

Picking up the binoculars, he scanned the horizon. He noticed the dust clouds first. Far off in the distance, but approaching at speed. The long column suggested at least five vehicles. They drove single file—pure arrogance. They expected minimal resistance. That was their first mistake. More would follow.

Bishop hit the button on his earpiece. "People, saddle up. We have company. Everyone in position." He eyed the line of black SUVs hurtling down the rough service road. "Showtime." Bishop ground his teeth. "Keep your heads, everyone. Stick to the plan. Take your time and shoot straight. And most importantly, drink plenty of water. I don't want anyone getting dehydrated out there."

The comms gear buzzed several times, as if someone was about to say something, then stopped. Li's voice came through hesitantly. "It's really hard to figure out if you're serious or crazy sometimes."

Smiling, Bishop hefted the sniper's rifle and tucked it into his shoulder. "I think you'll find, Li," Bishop tracked the lead vehicle and aimed the scope ahead of the convoy, where he'd partially buried an anti-tank guided missile by the side of the road, "that I'm most certainly both." He let out a breath and steadied his aim. "Here comes the big bang."

Tessa cut in. "Not the first time he's said those words."

Instead of replying, Bishop fired. The last SUV exploded. The rear of the vehicle rocketed upwards and a dirty orange fireball belched into the sky. Bishop hadn't had time to rig a pressure sensor to take out a car. Firing on an active anti-tank missile was the next best thing. And just as effective.

The convoy skidded to a halt. Three men piled out of the second-last vehicle to search for survivors. They scrambled down the embankment and walked alongside the makeshift road. That was their second mistake.

The lead man held his rifle tucked into his shoulder, sweeping for further AT mines at eye level along the roadway. He was looking in the wrong direction. He stepped forward and, seconds later, exploded when the landmine detonated. The man beside him fell and didn't move. The third limped back to his vehicle.

For the next minute, nothing happened.

"What are they doing?" Li's question was a valid one.

Bishop didn't take his eyes off the convoy. "Right now, they're figuring out how trapped they are. They can't go back—we just blew the only access road. They can't drive around, because now they know we've put landmines circling their position. They only have one choice."

Bishop detected movement. Four men exited the lead vehicle on the far side and stepped into the second.

Clutching the binoculars, Bishop grinned. "Chang's in the second vehicle now. Repeat, Chang is in vehicle two."

"Why'd he change cars?" Tessa asked.

"The first guy is what you call cannon fodder." Argento's tone was calm. "They probably think the road's mined. If there are more landmines, he'll be the first to find them."

"But the last car was the one Charles took out. It wasn't even a landmine."

"The gent in the front car doesn't know that. Jesus." Li let out a sigh. "That dude better be getting hazard pay, he'd be sweating bullets right about now."

They watched the first vehicle edge forward cautiously while the others held back and carefully followed its tyre marks. There was no need for Bishop to watch the procession. He wanted them to enter the city. In fact, his plan depended on it.

Leaving his post, he raced down the stairs. "You in position, Team Pink Bikini?"

"Affirmative, Team Tight Buns." Tessa giggled.

There was a sigh, and Argento's gruff voice cut in. "Can I once again object to these absurd team names?"

"No, you may not, Team Get Off My Lawn."

"For the record, Team Sequins here is fine with his name." Li's tone grew serious. "The lead guy is about to head up the embankment, folks. Time to drop those panties, y'all."

"Whatever happened to professional decorum?" There was no amusement in Argento's words.

"You picked the wrong crowd for that, baby."

"Evidently." Argento grunted. "Did you just call me baby?"

"Yo, yo." Li ignored the question and spoke excitedly. "First vehicle in. You're up, Team Bikini."

"Team *Pink* Bikini, thank you. On it."

Tessa's job was to count the assailants in the cars, and note their relative positions in the vehicles and how low each car was riding, indicating additional armaments or load. Everyone, Tessa included, knew it was the safest task. Bishop was keeping her away from harm.

Barely raising a sweat, Bishop reached the bottom of the stairs and ran into the city square, far from the view of the encroaching enemy. In the austere surrounds of the city's unused offices, nothing stirred. His footfalls echoed around the silent brick walls, amplified by the lack of trees and daily life, which would normally absorb sound. That was exactly what Li was working on, but it should have happened by now.

Sprinting into the municipal building, Bishop found Li behind the main counter in front of an open IT cabinet. "Have you hooked into the public address system?"

Li jumped. "Fucking hell, dude, you almost scared me straight."

"Why aren't I hearing music, Li?"

He waved his mobile phone at Bishop. "I'm connected to the PA, no worries. It's just… I can't…"

"Can't what?"

"I can't choose what to play, man. I want something epic, yeah? Like, I could put on Paul van Dyk, the man's a genius, but he's a bit clinical, right? Armin van Buuren?" He clicked his fingers. "Oooh, maybe classic

Tiësto, I don't know. Or what about some Israeli dubstep, just to fuck with 'em?"

Bishop grabbed Li's phone and typed. It took all of five seconds to pick something. He handed the phone back.

Li glanced at the screen and gawped, alarmed. "Are you fucking kidding me?"

Bishop pointed at the phone. "Put it on endless repeat, then get to your next position. You're cutting it fine."

As Bishop ran out of the reception area, Li shouted after him, "You're one evil son-of-a-bitch!"

Smiling, Bishop hit the square and ran towards the southernmost building. "Sitrep, Team Pink Bikini?"

"Last SUV coming into view now. They're maintaining tight formation. Driving west, sticking to route 3. Total assault team, eighteen. Six in the rear, four in the third, seven in the second, still one in the lead. All evenly loaded. They're…"

Amplified music came over the loudspeakers. "*I'll drive a million miles. To be with you tonight. So if you're feeling low. Turn up your radio…*"

Tessa continued. "They're travelling at… wait… is that Wang Chung? You're playing Wang Chung?"

"What's a Wang Chung?" Argento didn't seem amused.

"I'm pretty sure that goes against the Geneva Convention, Team Tight Buns."

"It's a classic. Everyone loves a classic." Bishop crossed the square and opened the door to the stairwell. "We could be easily discovered in the silence. This gives us cover." He ran up the stairs. "Plus, it's really annoying."

"*Everybody have fun tonight. Everybody have fun tonight. Everybody Wang Chung tonight.*"

"For the first time I wholeheartedly agree with you, son."

"You ready, Team Get Off My Lawn?"

"Look… yes, you little shit."

"Team Pink Bikini, ETA of the convoy passing Team Get Off My Lawn?"

Argento sighed.

"Give it twenty seconds. Leaving my visual. Going to second position."

"One of my favourites." Bishop grinned as they reached the roof of the car park.

"That's enough, you two." Argento left his comms open. "I have them. They're… they're slowing down. Is anyone in the open?"

"Negative."

"Negative."

"Nope."

"Well, something's spooked—heads up. All the doors just opened. They're all exiting the vehicles, sprinting for cover. They're splitting up. Repeat, they're splitting up. I can't get a clean shot."

"Acknowledged, Team Get Off My Lawn. How many left in the cars?"

"Just the drivers. Four. Plus two more standing guard."

"Right." Bishop inhaled deeply. "Time to go Cortés on their arses. Take out their escape, if you will, Team Get Off My Lawn."

"With pleasure."

From the top floor of the adjacent strip of shops, a streak of white smoke flew across the short distance to the first SUV. It exploded in flames, careening backwards into the car behind. Before the men on the ground could react, Argento fired the second rocket launcher and took out the third vehicle. The two guards tasked with protecting the convoy lay on the ground, motionless. Argento reloaded the first launcher, hefted it on his shoulder and took out the rear vehicle. The remaining driver, the one in the second vehicle, hadn't extracted himself from the SUV. He may have been pinned in place by the impact of the first rocket, possibly already dead. Argento would make sure of it. As the final streak of white crossed the sky, a smattering of Chang's men fired on Argento's position. But it was too late. For one, Argento was already gone. And with the final vehicle gone, they had destroyed Chang's only means of escape.

They'd also narrowed down the odds. The four now faced a dozen. They had prepared. They'd designed. They'd boobytrapped. They had a plan. It was now a game of odds. But Bishop's team also confronted the unknown. The enemy would no longer be complacent.

Without waiting for anyone's reaction, Bishop spoke unemotionally. "Everyone, enact protocol four. Go now."

Over the comms, Bishop heard overlapping movement. Li, Argento and Tessa were all changing position. For the next two minutes, he sprinted. Now the real danger began. They had a dozen targets, instead of four large ones. Things had become more complicated. And deadly.

He knew where each member of his team would be. Tessa was furthest from the engagement, heading east, towards the large apartment complex. They'd found a penthouse with a panic room; she'd been told to hold out there. Li was heading south-east, to the top of an incomplete water park. He would be their eyes in the sky now that Chang's men had entered the centre of the city. Argento would be traversing the roof between the shops and the nearby offices. He'd be converging on Bishop's position any second now.

Running through the entrance of the mall, Bishop

raised his pistol. There hadn't been enough time for any of Chang's men to have made it this far, but he wasn't taking chances. The mall was unfinished. Barely any interior fixtures had been completed, there were just bare concrete walls and exposed wiring. It was a husk, waiting for customers who may never come.

Bishop slipped through a concealed doorway, behind a pile of plaster leaning against a wall. Careful to leave the drywall in place, Bishop slid through the entrance to an access tunnel and ran on.

The white painted cinder blocks of the hallway concealed him from Chang's goons and allowed Bishop and Argento free movement between their designated positions. Sprinting, Bishop saw Argento ahead of him, doing his best to run but struggling. He didn't move like he used to. The younger man slowed and jogged alongside him.

"Want a race, old man?"

Argento huffed and kept running. "What are you doing, son? Team Pink Bikini?" He shook his head and coughed. "Who instructed you to run an operation like that? What are you playing at?"

Bishop rounded on Argento and the two men halted. He stared his old mentor in the eye as the old man puffed. "I'm not playing at anything, Kevin. What I'm doing is adjusting the parameters of the operation to ensure success. Tessa and Li, they're not operatives, they're scared stiff. I'm providing them with a psychological shield. I'm giving them cute team names to try to keep their minds off the fact that before the day is out, they will kill people. Real people. They're going to have to live with that. Until then, I'm doing my best to keep their minds off it. That's what I'm playing at." Bishop turned and walked on.

"Ah, I see. I hadn't taken that possibility into

account." Argento nodded and followed Bishop down the hall. "Seems you've learnt some things since our time. Very good. Carry on."

"Will do, Team Get Off—"

"Fuck off, you little shit!" Argento smiled as he did his best to match Bishop's increased pace.

It was good to share a joke with his old mentor. It had been many years. Regardless of the circumstances, it was nice to be working beside him again. Bishop just hoped they'd survive to reminisce about it one day.

A hesitant voice came over the comms. "Ah, Bishop…"

"Hey, no names, remember, Team Sequins."

In the background, Bishop could vaguely hear the words, *'Rip it up. Move down. Rip it up. Move it down to the ground.'*

Bishop shouldn't be able to hear the PA system from where Li was. Why was he out in the open? He should be in position by now. He should be…

"Yeah, about that…"

There was shuffling over the comms, as if the microphone was being dragged around.

A new voice came on. A colder voice. "Good afternoon, Bishop. It seems I've underestimated you again."

"Chang. Listen, the kid isn't even an operative. He works in IT. Spare him."

"Like you did my men in the cars? Or the amusement park? Or the van? You will pardon me if I'm in a less than forgiving mood, won't you?" Chang inhaled. "Where is she?"

"Amelia Earhart? I honestly don't know. I once met a bloke in the pub who swore she had a pie shop in Northampton. Or was it Worcester?"

The gunshot made Bishop jump. The ensuing silence chilled him to the bone.

"Jesus fuck, dude. That was right in my ear. If I'm deaf I'm suing, yeah?"

"That was the first and final warning shot, Bishop." Chang's voice was devoid of all emotion. "The next will be in his forehead. Where is she? You have five seconds."

Of course Chang would value Zhao over the nuclear case. Bishop had seen their bond in the van. In fact, he'd counted on it, only not so soon and not like this. He couldn't imagine how Li had been intercepted, but it could have happened in a million ways. The kid could have taken a wrong turn, one of Chang's goons could have been faster than they'd anticipated. It didn't matter now. Bishop had to keep him safe.

"Okay." He sighed. "Okay. I will tell you where she's held, but you have to guarantee the safety of the kid."

Bishop clicked his fingers and motioned for Argento to get into his next position. If Chang was heading to Zhao, they had to be ready. Argento nodded and sped off.

Bishop went on. "Do we have a deal?"

"Sure."

"You don't sound terribly convincing, Chang."

"Being convincing isn't my job, it's yours." A chill entered his voice. "Where is she?"

"Southern apartment block. Across from the square where the offices and shopping mall meet. Fourth floor, second apartment on the left, forty-eight. Now let him—"

The shot was as loud as it was sudden. The silence was thunderous. Bishop couldn't breathe.

"Chang?" He received no answer. "Chang?" Bishop pushed the earpiece further into his ear. "Li!"

No one spoke.

The only sound was faint pop music. *"Across the nation. Around the world. Everybody have fun tonight. A celebration so spread the word."*

The rest of the world was silent.

There was a buzz over the comms line. "I… I saw it. I saw him die. He's… Li's dead." The trembling voice descended into sobs.

"Tessa? Get off the channel." Argento's voice was harsh.

"Tessa Argento?" Bishop could hear the glee in Chang's voice. "Your daughter is here?" His laugh was as callous as it was chilling. "You better run, you MI6 bastards. I'm coming for you all. And Argento, you'll be last. You're going to see your little girl die before your eyes."

"Chang." Bishop's teeth were clenched. "I've been playing nice so far. That ends now. You're dead, you're just not buried yet."

"To be determined, Englishman. To be determined." Chang let out a sigh. "Let's finish this thing, shall we? I do recall saying this to you before, but now it carries so much more weight. You're going to beg for your life, Bishop."

"You first." Bishop broke into a run.

CHAPTER FOURTEEN

"Everyone switch to the alternate channel, now."

"Leaving so soon? I was only—" Chang's smug voice cut out when Bishop changed the frequency on his comms device.

"Tessa? Tessa, you there?" Bishop was out of breath, but it wasn't from running. Static filled his earpiece. "Tessa?"

"They… they just shot him. In the middle of the street, they just shot him. I've never seen anyone… I want to go home, Charles. Please can we go home?"

"Soon, baby, soon." He reached the end of the access tunnel where Argento stood. His old mentor's face mirrored the remorse and pain Bishop felt. On the other side of the wall was the street where Li's body lay. Bishop placed a palm on the wall and did his best to shut it out. He had to protect the living. "We have to take care of a few things first." *Like killing Chang's men, especially the man himself.* "Soon, I promise."

"Okay." Her voice seemed tiny.

"You stay with me, Poppet." Argento's voice was the opposite: strong and commanding. "You have the two most determined folks on the planet to keep you safe. Get to your position and stay there, you hear me?"

"Okay, Dad." She sounded defeated, on her last legs.

"You ready, son?"

Yanking the door open at the end of the tunnel, Bishop ground his teeth. "More than you know. We stick to the plan."

"It's a good plan."

Bishop turned to his old mentor. "Wait… did you just compliment me? You feeling okay?"

"Let's not push it, shall we?" The faintest grin creased the edges of his mouth. "Let's go. We do this for the kid."

The two men leapt through the door and into a loading dock. At least, it would have been a loading dock if the mall had ever been finished. It was, like the rest of the building, an empty industrial shell. But what it lacked in finish, it made up for in positioning. It was directly opposite the apartment Bishop had directed Chang to. The two men hid behind a recess built for dumpsters.

Bishop watched the footage on his phone, via the hidden cameras he'd placed earlier. Zhao appeared in the left window of the apartment, beating on the window, screaming. That would have been a confronting sight for Chang. On the far right, Bishop saw six men rush through the apartment entrance, submachine guns up.

Bishop watched the last man enter. "What did we time it at?"

"Thirty seconds flat." Argento checked his watch. "And mark."

For the next half a minute, neither man spoke. On his phone, Bishop saw Chang's men approach the apartment door. The men covered all access points professionally. They knew what they were doing. The second-last man carried something large.

"Is that a…" Argento squinted at the screen. "Where the hell did he get that?"

The man stepped forward, started a chainsaw and sliced through the apartment wall. It was a smart move. Doors could be boobytrapped, and it would be time-consuming to disarm any devices attached. Going through cheap timber and plaster was far easier. It was a shame they were wasting their time.

In another ten seconds, they were through. Shouting commands, they vaulted into the newly formed breach. Opposite the commotion, Bishop and Argento heaved rocket launchers onto their shoulders. Without uttering a command, both men fired.

The resultant explosions decimated the apartment and Chang's men, and also took out a good portion of the fourth floor of the building. The roof crumbled and chunks of concrete split away. The TV that had projected the false image of Zhao at the window fell to the road below.

The two men didn't wait; the trail from their weapons would be easy to follow. They ran back the way they'd come, through the tunnel of the shopping mall.

As he sprinted, Bishop switched comms channels. "You still with us, Chang?"

For several seconds, there was nothing but, "*Every-body have fun tonight, everybody Wang Chung tonight. Every-body have fun tonight, everybody have fun.*"

On receiving no reply, Bishop tried again. "Oh, and let's not forget your precious case, hey? You still want that too, right? What would you say if I said the case and the real Zhao were in the same place?"

"I would not believe anything you had to say, you hóng máo guǐzi, tǔbāozi nóng!"

"Woah there, big guy. Just trying to help."

"I will kill you!"

"Uh-huh, Sure. Listen, if you or any of your... let's see, four remaining guys, want to have a rest, there's a bar around the corner—"

The comms went dead.

Argento slowed, and put his hands on his knees. "You have a unique way of pissing people off, you know that?"

"Oh, absolutely. It's one of my key strengths. Along with my beer pong skills." Bishop grinned. "When he's pissed, he makes mistakes. Chang's temper is his greatest weakness."

"Shame he met you."

"Right? If he ever challenged me to beer pong he'd be so fucked."

Argento straightened his back. "See, you act like an idiot, but you're actually a damn fine agent."

"Let's not get ahead of ourselves, shall we? We're still outnumbered, and we've run out of rabbits to pull out of our hat. Let's get in our final positions."

"Then what?"

"Then I do what I do best of all."

Argento tilted his head. "Which is?"

"Be a blunt instrument." Bishop's face hardened. "He's going to pay for Li. For Ashley. For Ying Yue. For everything."

The two men ran on. Well, one ran, the other hobbled.

Nothing appeared in Bishop's sniper scope. Not that he expected it to. Chang had learned and adapted. He'd finally realised he wasn't in control, that his foes were far more capable than he had originally anticipated. That lesson came at a price. Wisely, he and his remaining men stuck to the shadows, out of sight.

Mostly.

Argento and Bishop had stumbled upon two of Chang's henchmen setting a tripwire at the entrance of the mall. Fortunately, the MI6 men had the jump on them. Those two had been dispatched with knives. Bishop's clothes were stained with their blood.

But for the last hour and a half there had been no sign of Chang or his remaining men. Nothing. Stalemate.

But not for long. The sun would be setting soon. That meant visibility was fading. Unfortunately, the stash of munitions they'd raided didn't include night-vision goggles. It was entirely possible Chang's men were equipped with some. Hell, they had a chainsaw. That could tip the balance in their favour. Bishop couldn't let that happen, so he had to take them down before the sun did the same. Their last play was thoroughly improvised. It wasn't pretty, but it would have to do.

Bishop was positioned above the cinema. He had removed several bricks and lay on his stomach, below the edge of the roof and out of sight. He swivelled his rifle and viewed the bait once more. Tethered to the empty fountain by the edge of the central square, Zhao stood like a sacrificial lamb. By her bound feet was the nuclear case.

She'd grown hoarse screaming blue murder at Bishop and Argento. Her exhausted form was now slumped against the hard grey bricks of a fountain that had likely never seen flowing water. It was an obvious trap, but even they served a purpose. The smart move would be to wait until nightfall, but one thing Bishop had observed about Chang was that smart wasn't always his first move. He was often swayed by emotions. Seeing his prize pupil humiliated could spur him into rash action.

Bishop waited. All was quiet. Mostly.

"Rip it up. Cool down. Rip it up. Get out what's inside of you. Everybody have fun tonight."

There were times when Bishop's smart-arsed moves ended up slapping him in the face. The brief moment of self-deprecating amusement quickly descended into despondency. The memory of Bishop and Li choosing the song quickly led to the memory of Li being shot. Bishop knew he couldn't allow himself to dwell on the loss, not now. He had to remain focused or more of them would share the young man's fate. What Bishop did allow to remain was the anger. That he could use.

"Heads up." Argento's voice snapped him back into vigilance. "East corner."

It was directly opposite where Argento was stationed, on the roof of the offices on the west side of the square.

Bishop pivoted his sniper rifle. "Got him. You have a shot? He's under my threshold. I've got nothing."

"I... I don't..." Argento sighed. "I don't have a shot. Bishop, if he keeps straight on, the fountain's going to cover him. Repeat, negative on the shot!"

Through the reflection in an apartment window Bishop could see Chang's black-clad man in a crouched stance, readying himself for the brief sprint to the fountain. He seemed to have found the perfect spot, where neither Argento nor Bishop had a shot. Almost as if...

As if charged with electricity, Chang's man sprinted for the fountain. In his hands were a small set of bolt cutters. He was a fast bastard, he'd cover the short distance quickly.

"I'm going to try and take him anyway." Argento's voice was filled with doubt.

"Negative." Bishop tried to keep his voice calm. "This is just like Lisbon. Remember how that turned out?"

"I hear you. Fuck it, taking the shot anyway."

"Argento, no!"

The ex-MI6 agent fired. His shot hit the top left corner

of the fountain, chipping away a fraction of a brick. Zhao screamed, but Chang's man kept running.

Argento's position was pummelled by machine gun fire. Chang's remaining men had been waiting for them to reveal themselves. Brickwork disintegrated under the intense barrage. It was relentless. High-calibre rounds destroyed the concrete where Argento had been concealed.

"Argento!" Bishop screamed for his former mentor.

There was no response. Bishop lifted his weapon above the edge of the roof, exposing his position to the enemy. He swung his rifle around and took aim at the man hurriedly trying to free Zhao. A single squeeze of the trigger removed the man's head. With blood and brains streaked across her face, Zhao screamed like never before.

Just as when Argento had fired, Bishop's position was pounded by artillery. Masonry flew in all directions, and bigger armaments blew huge chunks away. He dropped his rifle and rolled away, abandoning his post. Once out of the direct line of fire, Bishop sped towards the stairs.

"Argento? Come in, Argento!"

A series of clicks buzzed in Bishop's earpiece. The sound was followed by a hideous gurgle and desperate gasping. Bishop knew that sound all too well. It was the sound of someone drowning in their own blood.

"Kevin. Stay with me buddy." He bounded down the stairs five at a time. "Stay with me. I'm heading to your position. Stay with me, man. Stay with me."

There was no reply.

"Click your comms if you can hear me, Kevin. Just one click."

There was no reply.

"Kevin!"

There was no reply.

Several seconds later, Bishop hit the ground floor. The cinema was similar to the shopping mall: no fixtures in place, just a husk of a building that may never be used. A pistol in each hand, Bishop ran towards the entrance and what would almost certainly be a hostile reception.

He inhaled deeply and holstered one gun. Extracting a tiny mirror from his pocket, Bishop placed it on the ground and used it to search the surrounding buildings for any sign of his foes. He saw none.

About to take his chances and sprint across the small road between the cinema and the car park he'd originally come through, Bishop detected movement. In the far corner, far from his position, another of Chang's men appeared to be readying himself to make a run for Zhao.

The distance was too great for Bishop to confidently take him out with a pistol. If the goon was quick, he'd free Zhao before Bishop was within range.

Chang's man sprinted into the square. He seemed even faster than the first. He made Zhao's position and took the bolt cutters from the hand of his headless comrade.

Bishop hit the button on his comms gear. "You have the shot?"

A hesitant and distant voice replied. "I… I do."

"You don't have to do this, Tessa. I understand if—"

The gunshot was amplified by the earpiece. Bishop watched Chang's man in the square. One moment he was furiously attempting to cut the chains around the fountain, the next he slumped to the ground, lifeless.

"Great shooting, Tessa." The girl could shoot, that was for sure. "Now stay still, keep your head down."

And then there was one. Chang was the only one of his assault team left. He could be anywhere. The man could not be underestimated. If he was unstable and dangerous before, that would be magnified exponentially now that he was cornered and alone. Bishop just hoped Tessa would remain out of sight long enough for him to take Chang out.

Chang would know it was just the two of them now. Mano a mano.

Closing his eyes to steady himself, Bishop prepared to sprint for Argento's position. The road was thin, he needed to weave his way over. He'd make it in a few seconds. Gripping his pistols tight, he took one final breath.

"Yoo-hoo! Mr Bishop!"

He didn't dare move. The shout was loud and from a distance. But there was something about the tone. Something smug.

Bishop's blood turned to ice. He twisted his head and shouted, "What do you want, Chang?"

"Your head!"

"I'm quite attached to it."

"Really? I'll trade you for it!"

In the distance Bishop could hear shuffling and scraping footsteps. He turned and froze.

Near the fountain, Chang ambled onto the road. He wasn't alone.

With a pistol to her temple, Tessa's face was streaked with tears. Whether they were for Li, her father or her predicament, Bishop couldn't tell.

Bishop strode onto the road and marched towards Chang.

"I only just put it together." Chang smiled as he pressed the gun to her head. "My men in London came across a most dangerous opponent who was protecting Tessa Argento. He very much meets your description, don't you think? My men said the two appeared to have a special bond." He pushed the gun harder into Tessa's temple. "I'm betting you won't do anything stupid here, Bishop."

"You don't know me at all if that's what you think, Chang." Bishop kept striding forward. "We're the only ones left." He nodded towards the pistols in his hands. "And we're both armed." Bishop aimed a pistol at Zhao.

Chang frowned. "My shot will definitely hit first, wouldn't you think?" His deranged eyes flared. "Or do you want to take the chance?"

Bishop stopped walking. "What do you want?"

"First of all," Chang inhaled deeply, "turn that fucking song off!"

"Wouldn't even if I could."

"But now the music's on. Oh baby dance with me yeah. Rip it up. Move down."

Studying her face, Bishop asked, "You okay, Tessa?"

She nodded, convincing no one.

"Just shoot the bitch!" Zhao's eyes were wild. The woman appeared unhinged.

"Now now, Zhao…"

"My name is not fucking Zhao!" Her head snapped around to her mentor. "Chang, kill the fucking slut and then shoot him!"

"Listen, Zhao," Bishop addressed her calmly, "I know you're upset because we didn't get to sleep together, but please be quiet. I'm trying to listen to Wang Chung."

"If I may interrupt?" Chang tapped Tessa's head with the barrel of the pistol to gain Bishop's attention. He'd pay for that.

Close to losing it, Tessa stared at Bishop, eyes wide and full of tears. "I… I want to go home, Charles."

"We will soon. Promise."

Chang puckered his brow. "You're in no position to make that promise, Englishman. You had your shot and you lost. You have no more cards to play. Now drop the guns. You are done."

Chang was right. All was lost. Despondent, Bishop tossed both his pistols to the ground.

Chang lowered his gaze menacingly. "Is there something you want to say to me?"

Bishop nodded. He sighed, defeated. "Carrot juice is technically orange juice."

Chang's face grew more agitated. "No, you know what I mean. I told you this time would come, didn't I? It's time for you to beg me for your life, Bishop."

Frowning, Bishop shrugged. "Why would I do that?"

Chang's face flushed red. "Because I'm the one holding the fucking gun!" He pushed Tessa to the ground and raised his pistol to Bishop. "Because—"

The crack was like thunder. It reverberated around the square. Chang dropped his pistol, staggered backwards and clutched his chest. More accurately, he clutched where his chest used to be. In his last seconds of life, Chang stared at the unarmed Bishop, his confusion absolute. He fell forward, lifeless.

Bishop ran towards Tessa and scooped her into his arms. She was half dazed.

"You're a madman, you know that right?"

"I've been called far worse."

She caressed his cheek. "I know. Mostly by me."

"You okay?" Bishop helped her up slowly.

"I will be." She frowned. "Eventually."

Bishop hit the button on his comms device. "Nice shooting, Kevin. Good to see you're not completely senile."

"I still have more bullets in this gun, you little shit."

"But..." Zhao was still chained to the fountain, confused. "But Argento is dead!"

Bishop shook his head. "No, he was playing dead. As

soon as we said over comms that we didn't have a shot, your man ran across the square. That's when we knew we were compromised. Chang's overconfidence cost him his life."

When Bishop had told Argento, "Just like Lisbon" it had been code. He'd been referring to a previous operation in Lisbon, where their comms network had been compromised. It had cost them good men that day. Now it had cost Chang everything.

It was over.

EPILOGUE

The city below sped by. Reclined in the passenger seat of the civilian Airbus Helicopters H160, Bishop found it impossible to relax. Not yet.

They were somewhere over Suzhou, on their way to the airport in Shanghai. MI6 assured him they would be wheels up in less than an hour. He wouldn't unclench until they were far from Chinese airspace. In front of him sat five intense-looking Royal Marines, armed to the teeth with weaponry and serious dispositions.

Bishop had insisted they take Li's body with them. It was currently stowed in the rear baggage compartment. The soldiers had originally claimed they only had orders to extract Bishop and the Argentos. That was when they discovered Bishop's determination in the face of bureaucracy. Once they realised the helicopter wouldn't be taking off without Li's body aboard, they made quick work of it.

Zhao would be subject to extraordinary rendition. Like Li, they faced a dilemma. She couldn't be left behind in the abandoned city, but at the same time, with all Zhao had done, rewarding her with a five-star luxury ride seemed an insult to those who had died. Bishop offered what he believed to be an elegant solution; the same as Li's. Currently Zhao was locked in the rear baggage compartment with the corpse, hopefully learning a valuable life lesson. Or not. Bishop was beyond caring at this point. He doubted she'd ever set foot on her home soil again. He found it impossible to feel sorry for her.

Beside him, Argento snored loudly. On his other side, Tessa was slowly coming out of her deep shock. She'd traversed a myriad of emotions as she struggled to come to terms with the last few hours. She'd seen life taken away, she'd taken a life herself. But she'd kept her head throughout. And her father was safe. It was a base she could build on.

Throughout the mission Bishop had done his best to ignore the rekindled emotions he felt for Tessa. He had to, for all their sakes. Now with Chang dead, his feelings seemed to have doubled down. He had to fold them up and place them in a box. The woman was distraught, emotionally and physically scarred. It was absurd to even acknowledge such feelings, not to mention utterly inappropriate.

He took one last look at the side of her beautiful face as she stared out the window, and then closed his eyes. He would board the plane, take a sleeping tablet and do his best to avoid her until they disembarked. Tessa deserved more than he could ever give her. He would need to keep repeating that mantra until he believed it.

Bishop sighed. He had been through so much in such a short period of time, it was hard to keep track of it all. As the first strands of sleep crept over his consciousness, a soft hand touched his arm.

He opened his eyes and turned. "Hey."

"Hey." For a brief second, Tessa's face was the same

one he remembered in his dreams. A radiant beacon of perfection. It lasted a fraction of a second before her face darkened, as if recalling what she'd been though. "Thank you. For rescuing Dad. Saving me. Everything."

"It wasn't enough. We lost too many."

"To save so many more. Really, thank you."

She leaned forward and kissed his cheek. Her face hovered, not retreating, then her lips brushed his. Their breath intertwined, Tessa edged forward and kissed him. He kissed her back. In mere seconds, their embrace heightened, their kiss intensified. Tessa's tongue sought his.

Just as quickly, she moved back, seemingly shocked at her actions. "I'm… I'm sorry, Charles."

"It's okay, Tessa. You've been through so much. I'm sorry to have—"

"I can't be with you, Charles. I'm sorry."

It felt like all the air had been sucked out of the helicopter.

Bishop nodded; he didn't know what else to do. "I understand."

"Look, shit, I'm sorry, I'm doing this all wrong. I shouldn't have kissed you, that was heartless. Sorry. Shit. Sorry." She buried her head in her hands.

He placed his hand on her shoulder. "Tessa, it's okay. Really. I understand."

"You don't." She raised her head. Her smile was sweet, but there was pain in her eyes. "But it's nice of you to say so."

"No, I actually do. We have a bond, we always have, even when we were yelling at one another in the middle of the night. That will never change. I've seen flashes of it again in the last few days—flashes, that's all. But you've realised we can't be together, not now. Not ever." Bishop was unsure who he was convincing, but he couldn't stop.

"You saw me, the real me today. What I'm capable of, the man I truly am. You can't reconcile that with the man you once knew. The one whose arms you fell asleep in, lying in front of the fireplace in Vienna." Bishop tilted his head inquisitively. "Pretty close?"

Tessa furrowed her brow. "When did you get so wise?"

"I've always been this wise, you were just distracted by my devilish good looks."

Rolling her eyes, Tessa slid her arm around Bishop and hugged him close. She gazed out the window, as if unable to look him in the eye. "Yes, I saw the unbridled, unshackled Charles Bishop. It was glorious. It was spectacular." She sighed. "It was terrifying. You're a force of nature, my love." She turned to him, her face the saddest he'd ever seen it. "But I can't tame that. I never could, nor would I want to. You don't want me." She held up a hand to fend off his argument before he'd even made it. "No, I should rephrase; you don't need me. You need someone who is your equal, someone who can either temper the fire within you or fan it so you both burn the world to the ground." She cupped his face in her hand. "But that's not me. I hope you find her, whoever she is. You deserve to be happy. I could never make you happy, Charles. Not really. I'd only hold you back and you'd ultimately resent me for it. Not now, maybe we'd have a few good years, but it would creep in, like a winter chill. It would kill us both in the end."

Bishop swallowed hard, unable to speak. Tears welling, he nodded.

Her face warmed and she gave him a sad smile. "She's out there, somewhere. You need to go find her."

Knowing he should answer, Bishop found himself unable to. He knew she was right, but the logic didn't cut through the pain. He had clung to the unrealistic hope that they would find a way. But Tessa was right, they never would. Bishop shivered. He suddenly felt cold. It was probably the ice shield around his heart reforming.

On his other side, Argento woke with a jolt. Bishop patted his arm.

"It's alright, Kevin. It's over."

The older man stretched. "I didn't expect to be alive at the end of this mission."

"You and me both, old man."

The two former friends nodded at one another.

"I meant what I said a few hours back." Argento rubbed his face. "You've lived up to the name I gave you."

"Partly gave me." Bishop gave him a roguish grin.

Argento nodded, conceding the point. "If my old man ever met you he'd be as proud as I am."

It was many years ago, when the man who would become Bishop was leaving the SAS. On signing his resignation letter, his commanding officer had sneered. "You can change organisations, shitheel, but you'll never escape your past. Once a cunt, always a cunt."

Despite being such a tough and weathered soldier, the remark cut him to the bone. The man who would become Bishop had not always stayed on the good and true path. Nathan Vincent's late teens had been rife with misdemeanours, theft and assaults. He was the very definition of a wayward teen, on his way to becoming a menace to society. He knew it, but had no capability to pull himself out of the downward spiral. One night he drunkenly attacked a man in a bar for some minor indiscretion Bishop couldn't even recall. The poor bastard had needed reconstructive surgery.

His only options were joining the army or jail. He'd made his choice, but the past had a way of catching up. A squad mate had been the first to find out. A friend of a friend heard Nathan's name and passed on the news. He was a thug who had escaped justice. From that day forward, he was persona non-grata in his platoon. The day Argento first saw him, Nathan was being beaten to a pulp in the boxing ring. He refused to stay down.

The SAS commanding officer's parting dig resonated with the young man for some time. He finally told Argento what had been bothering him. His mentor's response was both simple and revelatory. "Why not change your name? How many people get a chance to completely reinvent themselves?"

Nathan Vincent had been given that chance. He took it. But what name should he take?

His old mentor was there to help once more. The two sat on either side of a chess board, playing one of their famously long matches. "My father's name was Charles. He died two summers ago. He was a strong son of a bitch who had a misspent youth, too. I'd be honoured if you'd consider it."

The pupil could think of no greater compliment. "I'd be honoured." He moved his piece into place. "What about a last name?"

"That's for you to decide, I'd think."

The apprentice moved his rook and took Argento's bishop. Instead of placing it on the table, the young man rolled the piece in his hand.

Argento regarded him curiously. "What are you smiling at?"

The soon-to-be MI6 agent held up his opponent's chess piece and smiled.

Now, on the helicopter, recalling the memory, Bishop grinned. Tessa caught the expression and wrinkled her nose inquisitively.

"What's next for the great Charles Bishop?" she asked.

"Well," Bishop yawned, "I only have one real wish."

Argento tilted his head. "And what's that?"

"To get Wang Chung out of my head. It's driving me crazy."

THE END

ABOUT DAVE SINCLAIR

Dave Sinclair is a novelist, a screenwriter and a really excellent parallel parker.

He lives in Melbourne, Australia with his fiancé Kristi and two crazy daughters. He's also an award-winning filmmaker, a title that sounds far more impressive than it really is. He won a best comedy screenplay and cinematography award for a short film he wrote and directed, though at the time he didn't really know what cinematography was. A completed screenplay is currently doing the rounds.

Dave's overflowing bookshelves include many works by Douglas Adams, P.G. Wodehouse, Dashiell Hammett, Raymond Chandler, Janet Evanovich, Ian Fleming, Zadie Smith and John le Carré.

The Eva Destruction and Charles Bishop books are stories Dave wanted to read, full of action, laughs and fascinating characters.

To find out more, you can stalk Dave at his semi-reputable website: https://davesinclair.com.au

ACKNOWLEDGMENTS

This book scared me. It really did. I've written a few novels and every one of them – every single one – I've gotten about halfway through and hated it. Positively loathed it. But in writing *Agent Provocateur*, something changed. I didn't hate it once. It all just flowed. It was a weird experience to have a blast with a book from beginning to end. Hope you enjoyed the ride too!

Now for the acknowledgements!

First and always goes to my biggest supporter, my amazing fiancé Kristi. Her boundless belief in me keeps me going every day. Honestly, she's the reason you're reading a Bishop series at all. Thank you. Monkey heart unicorn, you're amazing.

To my girls, Quinn and Esther, thank you for supporting your crazy dad and telling all your teachers about my books, you're my little cheer squad. Avid readers, I can't wait until you're ready to read one of mine... let's just give it a few years, shall we?

raises a glass Here's to the G-Mob. Every writer needs a tribe. The G-Mob are amazing writers and even better friends. Craig, Justin, Luke, Nathan, Steve,

Amanda and Amanda have provided support, assistance, insight and laughter when I need it most. You should give them a read! http://genremob.com/

Did someone say sibling rivalry? No such thing. Here's to my talented sis, Alli, thank you for always being so amazingly supportive. Check out her novels – http://allisinclair.com. As you can tell from the dedication in this book, there's a lot of love.

A big thank you to my editor Vanessa Lanaway. She does an amazing job of making my words almost readable. No mean feat. She's also a great supporter of my writing, thank you.

Thanks to Amanda Pillar (a member of the G-Mob and a fantastic writer) who designed all the Bishop covers. Check out her cover work here – https://www.smokinghotcovers.com/

A big cheers to my beta readers, Steve & Gerard. Thanks for pointing out the plot holes I missed. Any that remain are completely their fault.

A big shout out to my VIP Book Club team who receive my exclusive newsletter. One lucky newsletter reader, Carol Gray, won a competition to have her appear in this book so she could be killed off (remember the Assistant Secretary of GCHQ?).

And to my amazing Book Ninjas who receive an advance copy of my novels – thank you for the amazing feedback! You guys rock.

Don't be afraid to reach out on Facebook, Twitter, Instagram. It's always great to hear from folks. You can stalk me at all these semi-reputable places:

www.davesinclair.com.au

https://twitter.com/thedavesinclair

https://www.instagram.com/davesinclairauthor/

https://facebook.com/DaveSinclairAuthor/

Finally, thank you to the readers. Don't be shy about

dropping a review, it is greatly appreciated, and it really helps people discover my work. Thank you and here's to many more adventures!

Until next time, remember, everyone have fun tonight, everyone Wang Chung tonight.